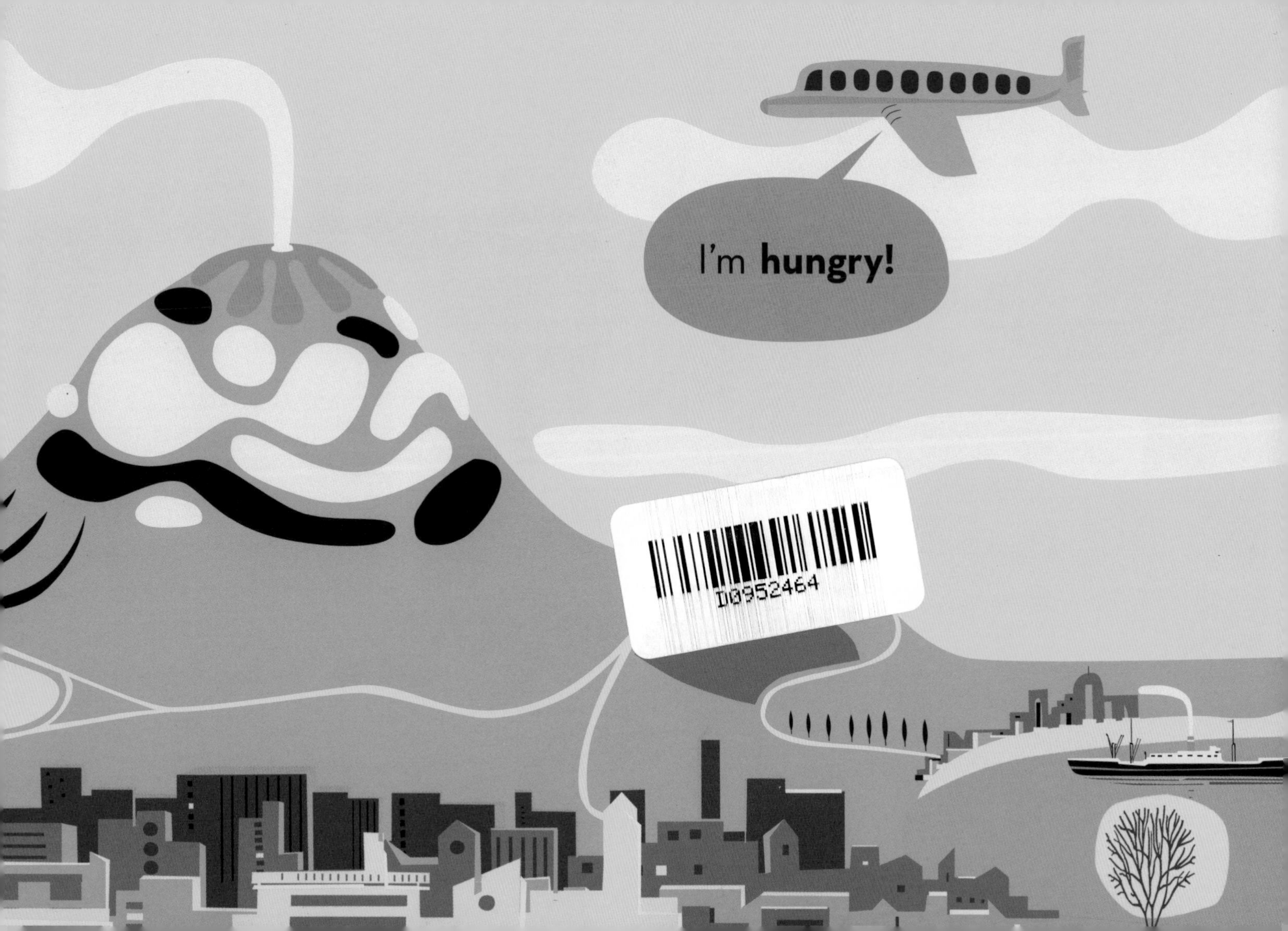
I'm **hungry!**

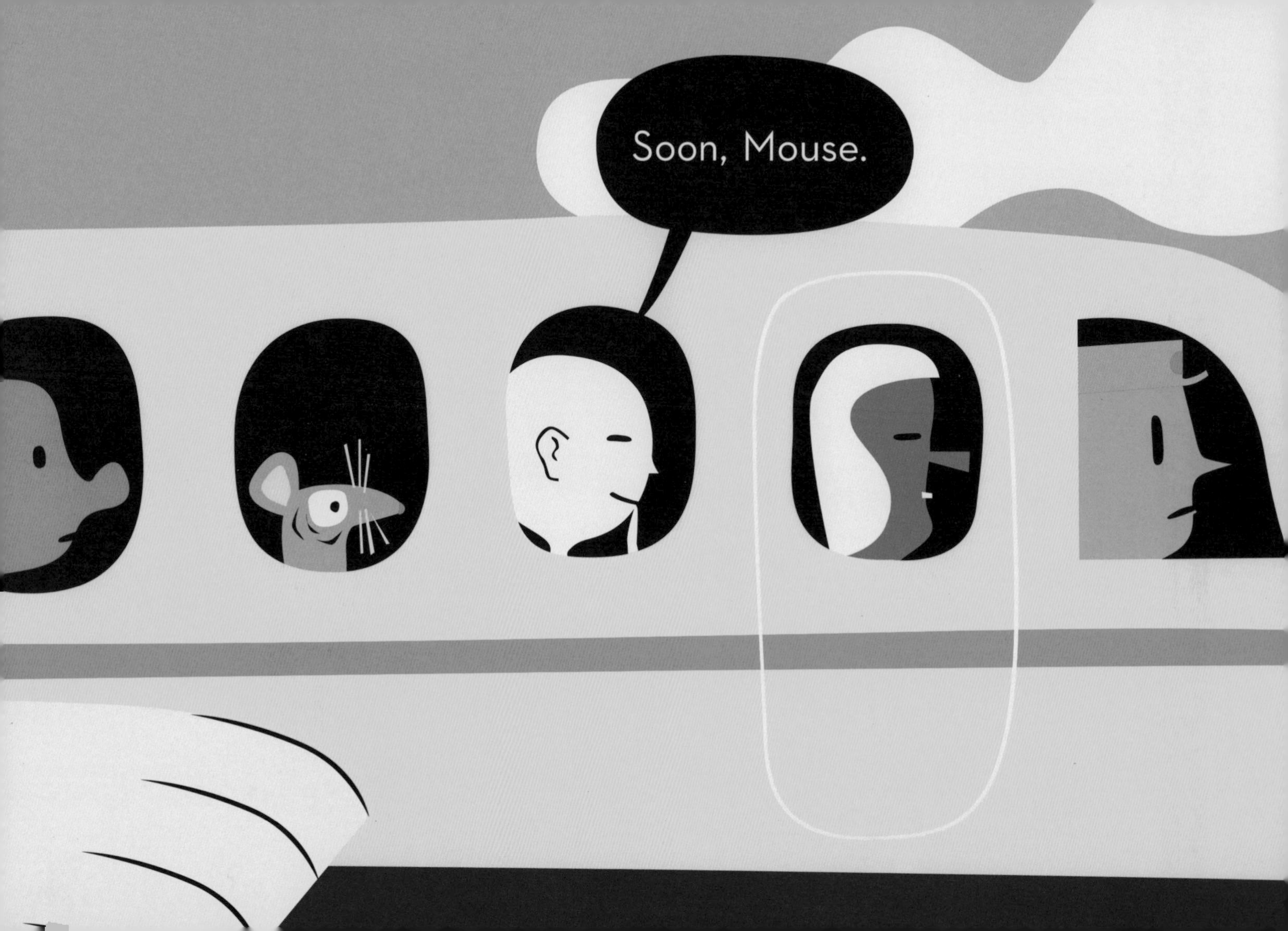
Soon, Mouse.

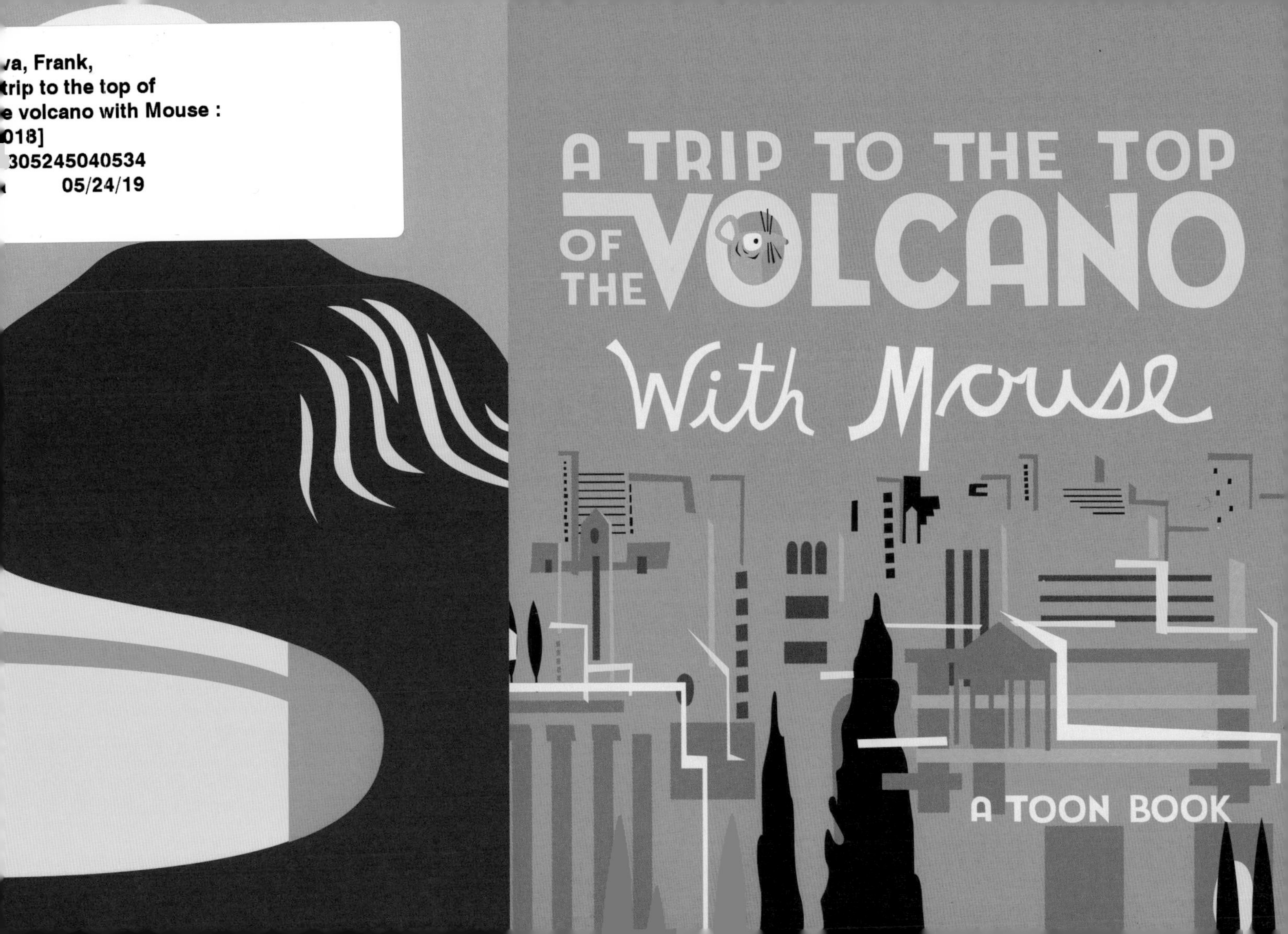
A TRIP TO THE TOP OF THE VOLCANO
With Mouse
A TOON BOOK

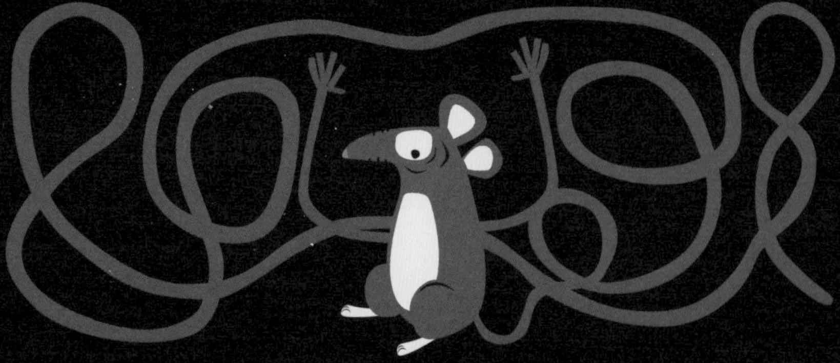

## A TOON BOOK

**Editorial Director:** FRANÇOISE MOULY
**Book Design:** FRANK VIVA and FRANÇOISE MOULY

FRANK VIVA's artwork was created using Adobe Illustrator. The words are set in Neutraface, and the display type is hand drawn by Frank Viva. All our books are Smyth Sewn (the highest library-quality binding available) and printed with soy-based inks on acid-free, woodfree paper harvested from responsible sources.

 Library of Congress Cataloging-in-Publication Data: Names: Viva, Frank, author, illustrator. Title: A trip to the top of the volcano with mouse: a TOON Book / by Frank Viva. Description: New York, NY: TOON Books, [2019] | Summary: "A boy and a mouse trek to the top of a volcano, taking in soaring trees, lunar landscapes, and snowcapped peaks, then return to the city at the bottom."—Provided by publisher. Identifiers: LCCN 2018001055 | Subjects: LCSH: Graphic novels. | CYAC: Graphic novels. | Volcanoes--Fiction. | Voyages and travels—Fiction. | Mice—Fiction. Classification: LCC PZ7.7.V59 Tt 2018 | DDC 741.5/973--dc23 | LC record available at https://lccn.loc.gov/2018001055. Printed in China by C&C Offset Printing Co., Ltd. Distributed to the trade by Consortium Book Sales & Distribution, a division of Ingram Content Group; orders (866) 400-5351; ips@ingramcontent.com; www.cbsd.com.

ISBN 978-1-943145-36-2 (hardcover)

19 20 21 22 23 24 C&C 10 9 8 7 6 5 4 3 2 1

TOON–BOOKS.COM

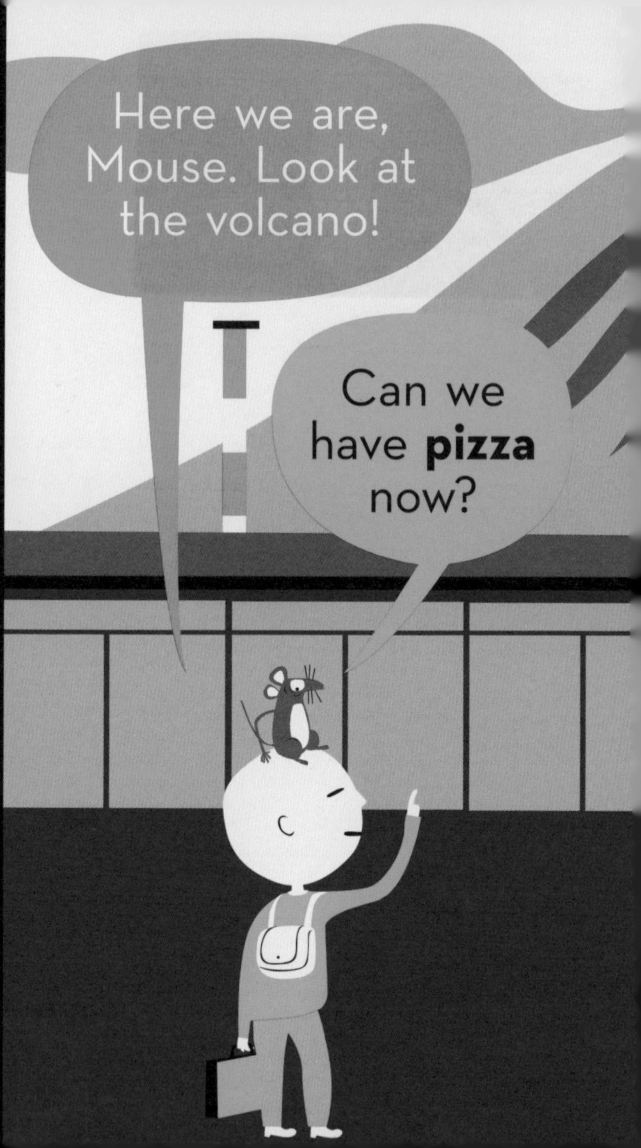
Here we are, Mouse. Look at the volcano!
Can we have **pizza** now?

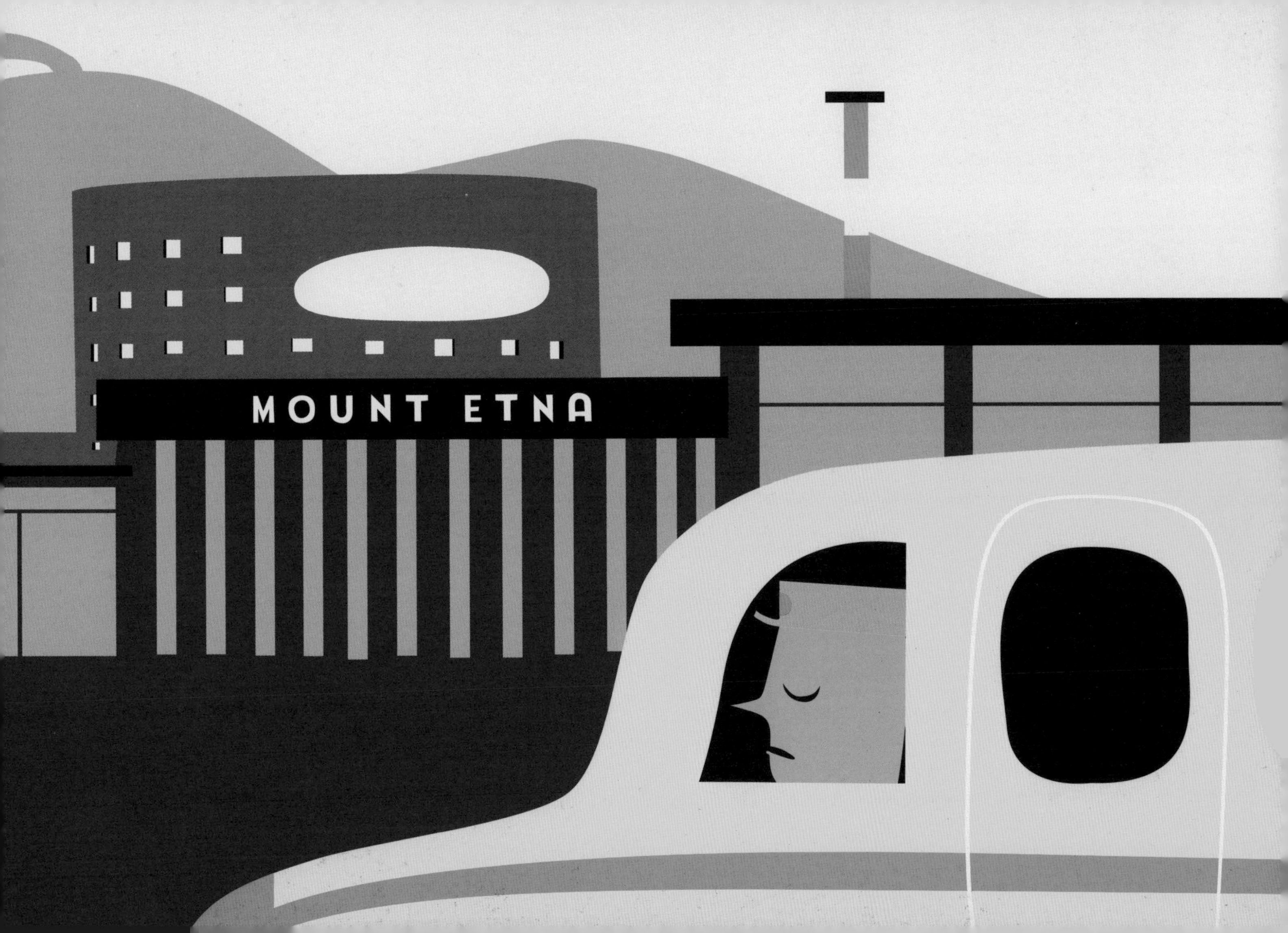
MOUNT ETNA

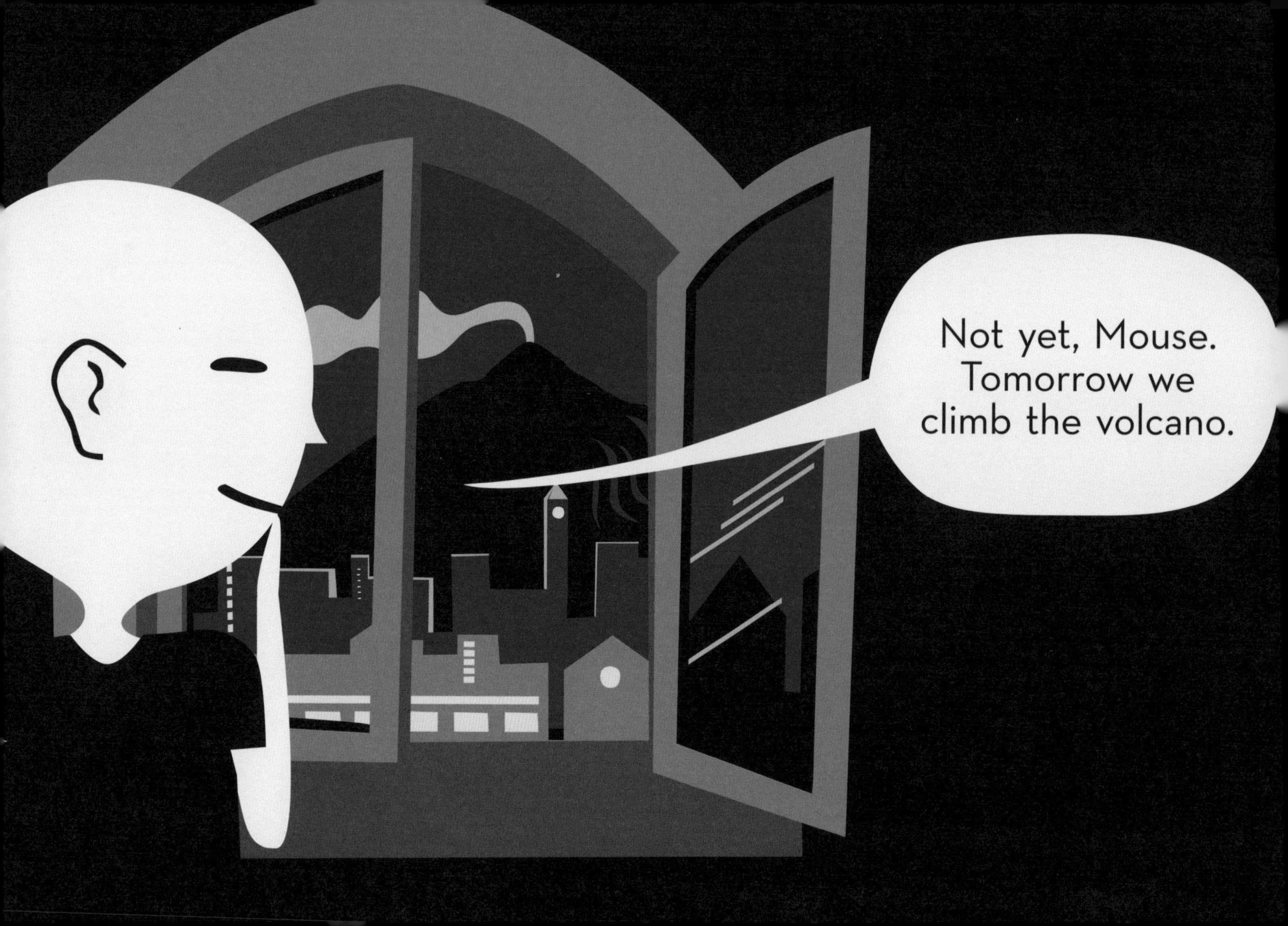
Not yet, Mouse. Tomorrow we climb the volcano.

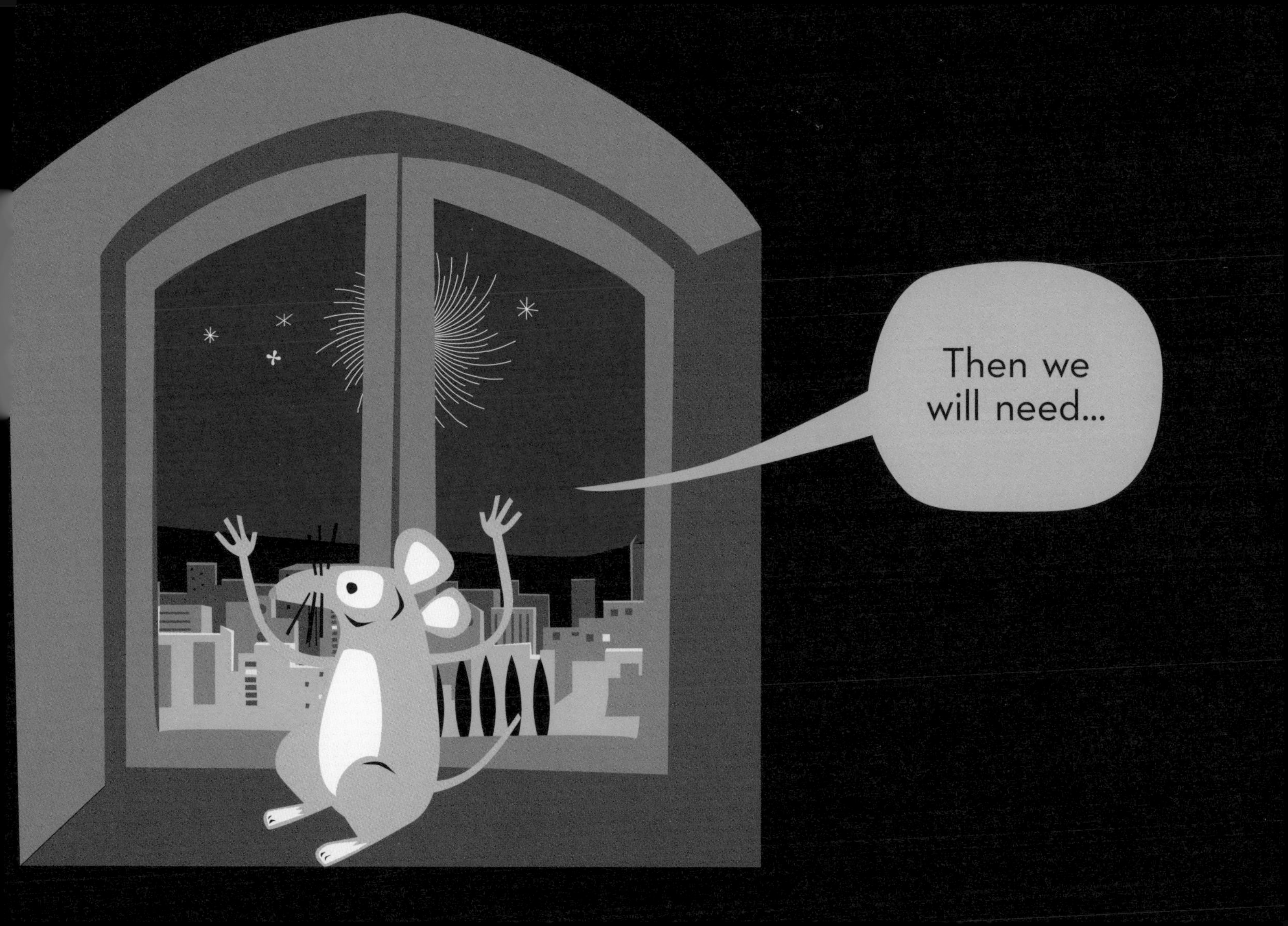
Then we will need...

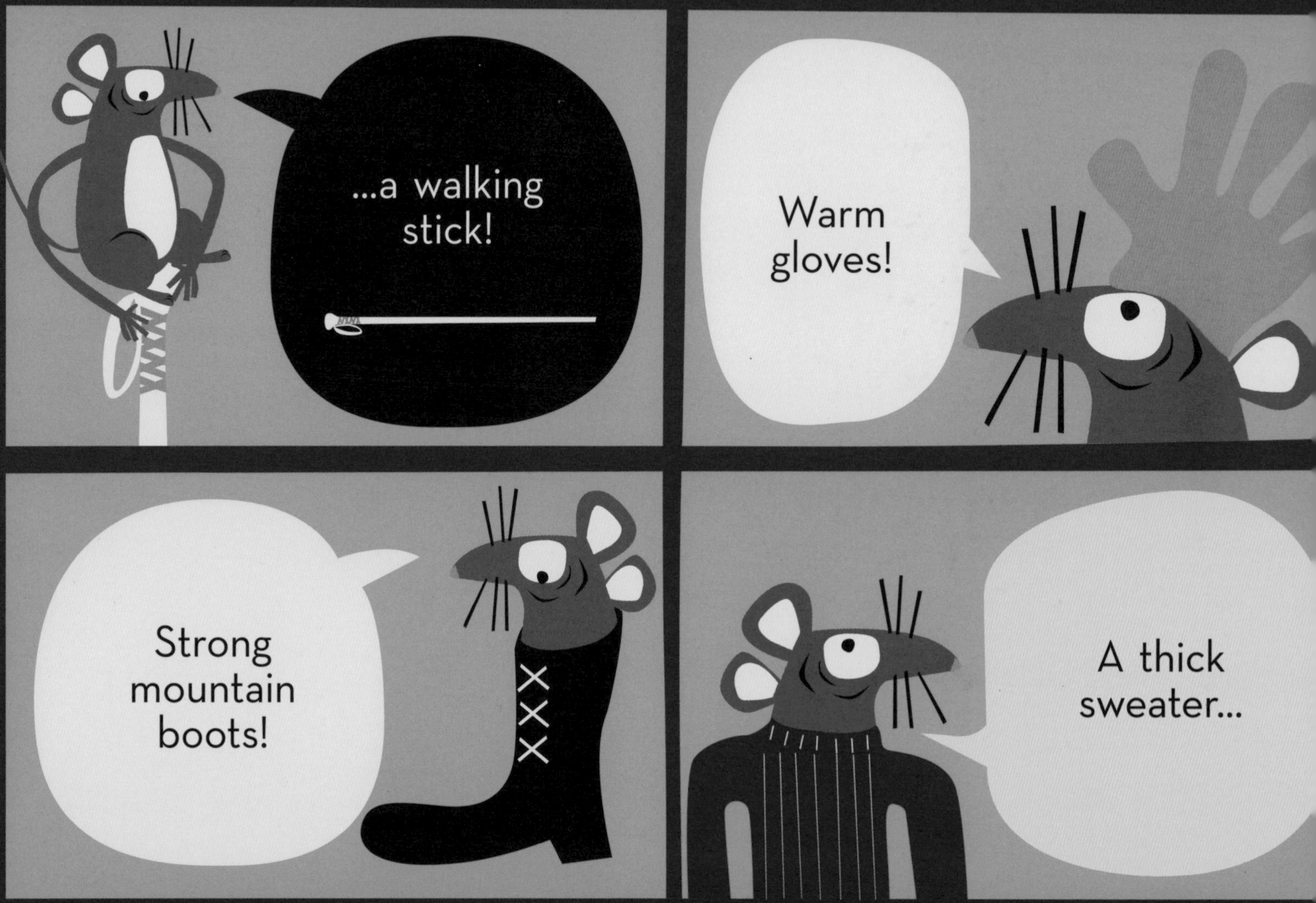
...a walking stick!
Warm gloves!
Strong mountain boots!
A thick sweater...

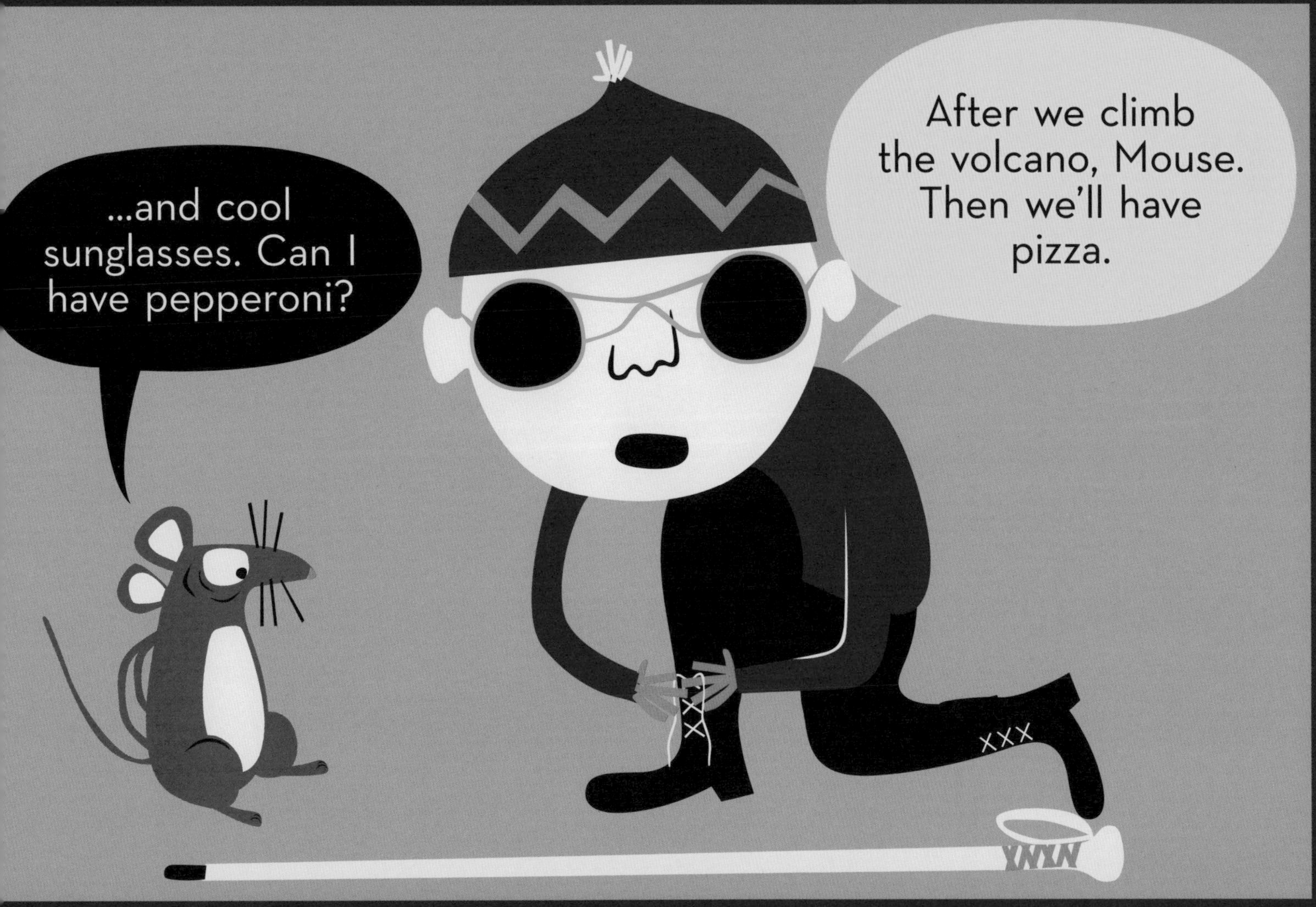
...and cool sunglasses. Can I have pepperoni?
After we climb the volcano, Mouse. Then we'll have pizza.

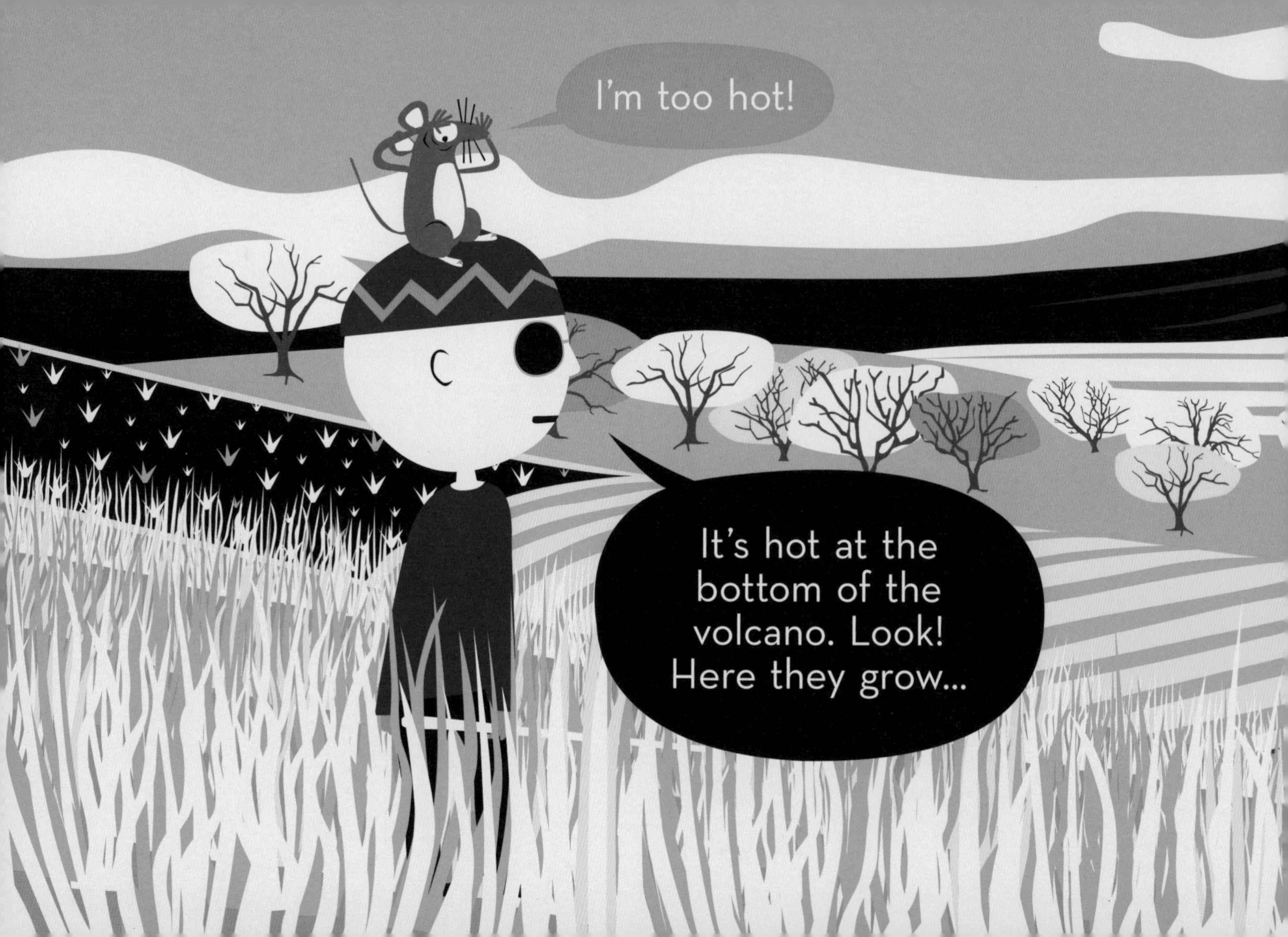
I'm too hot!
It's hot at the bottom of the volcano. Look! Here they grow...

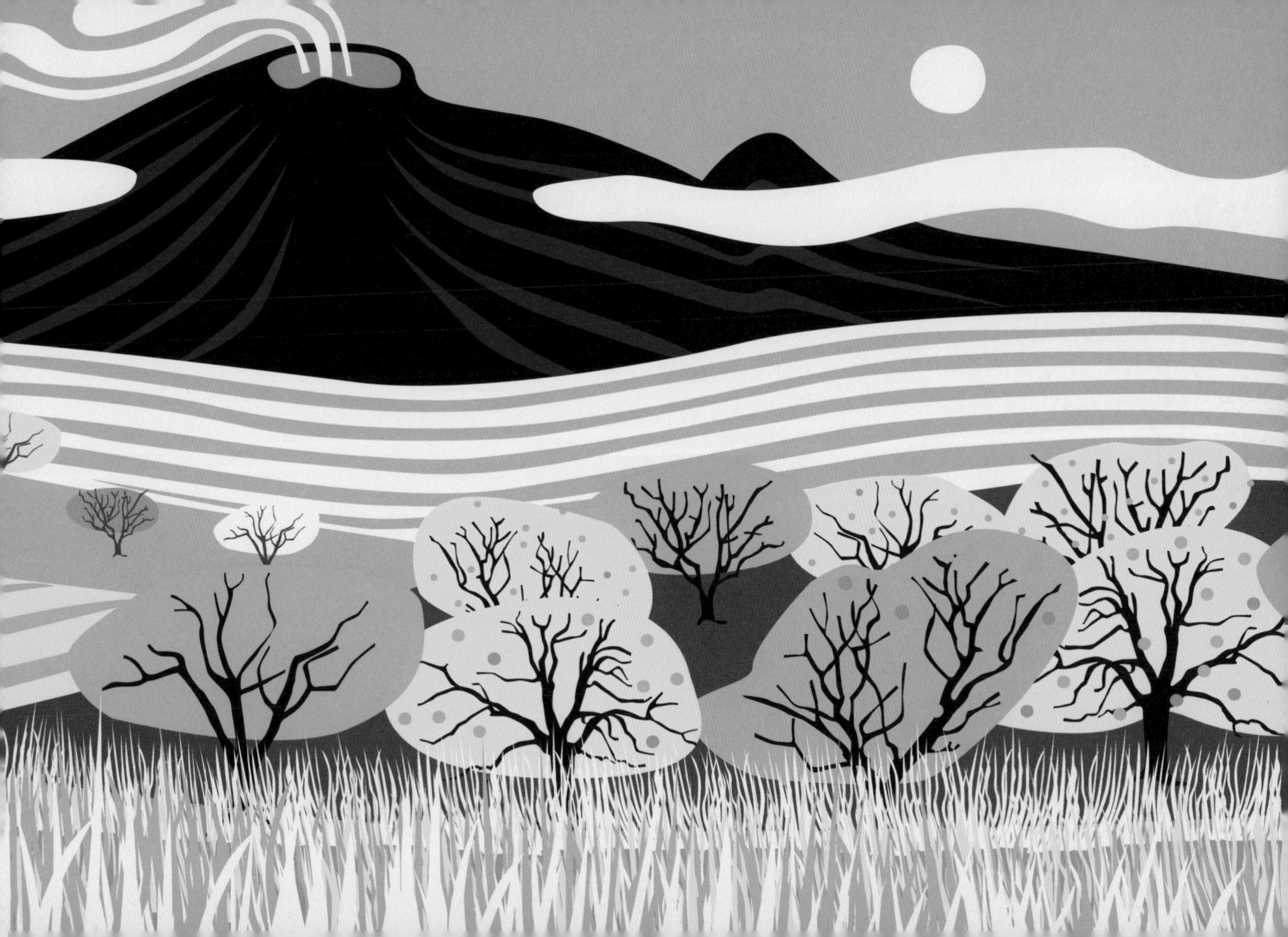

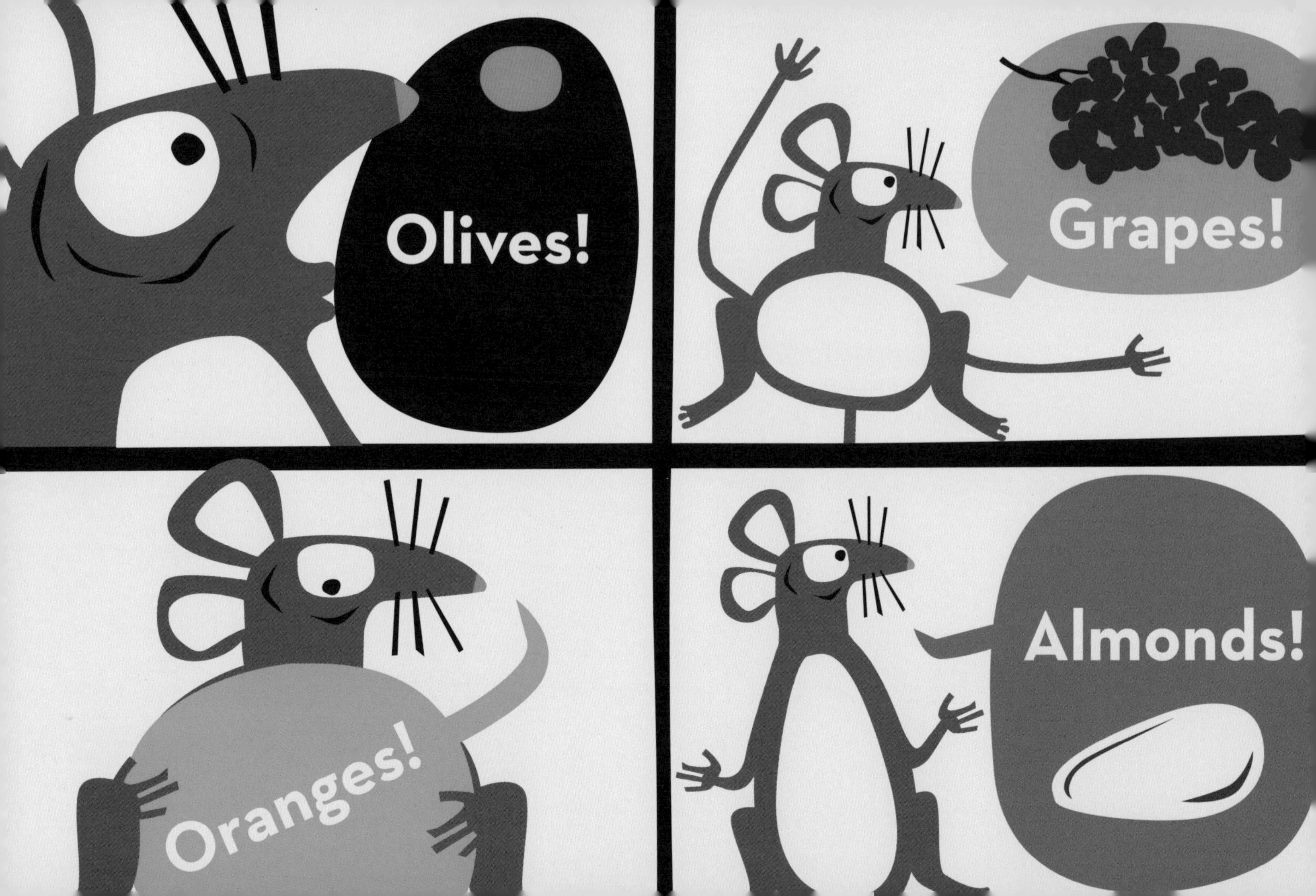
Olives!
Grapes!
Oranges!
Almonds!

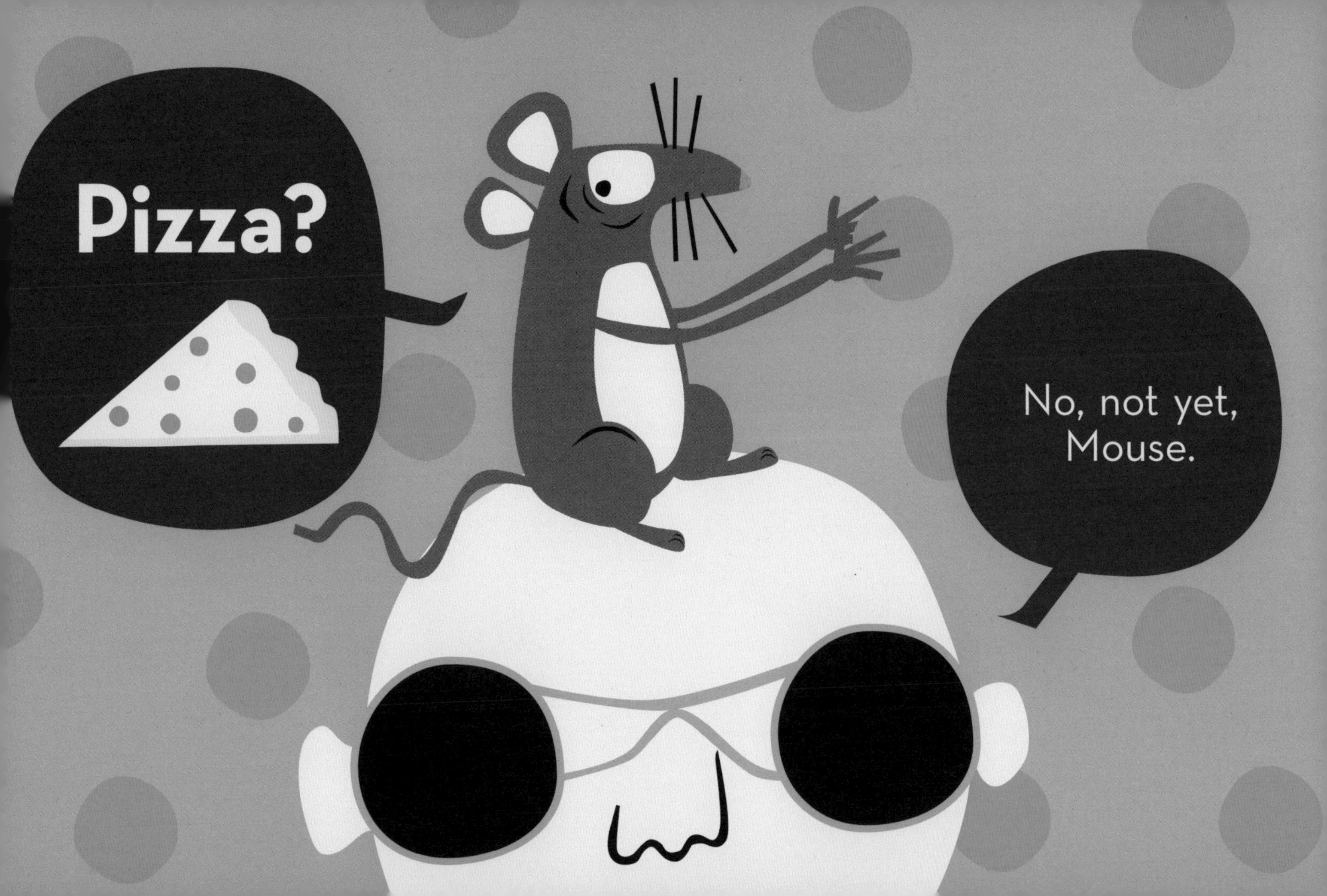
Pizza?
No, not yet, Mouse.

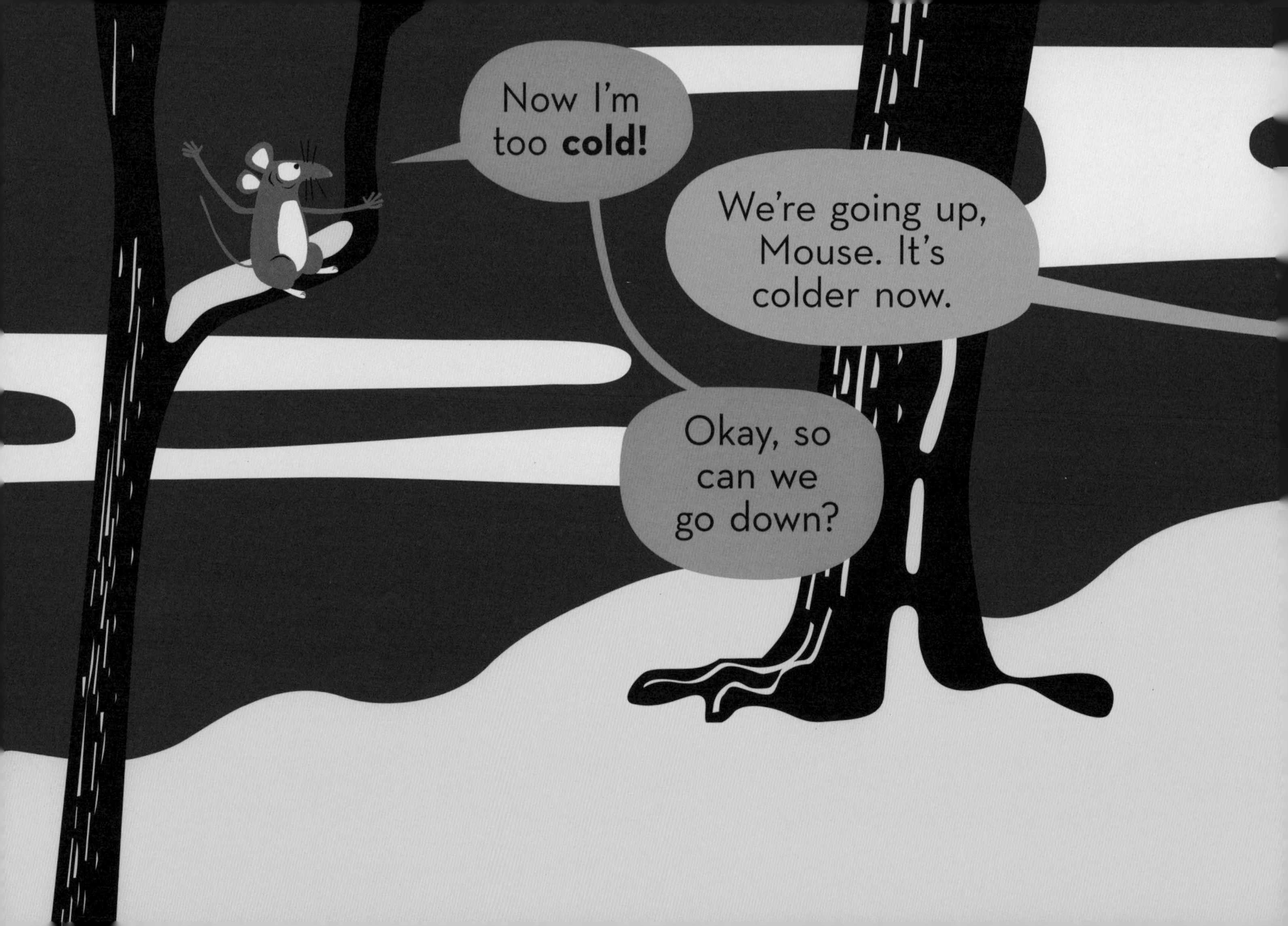
Now I'm too **cold!**
We're going up, Mouse. It's colder now.
Okay, so can we go down?

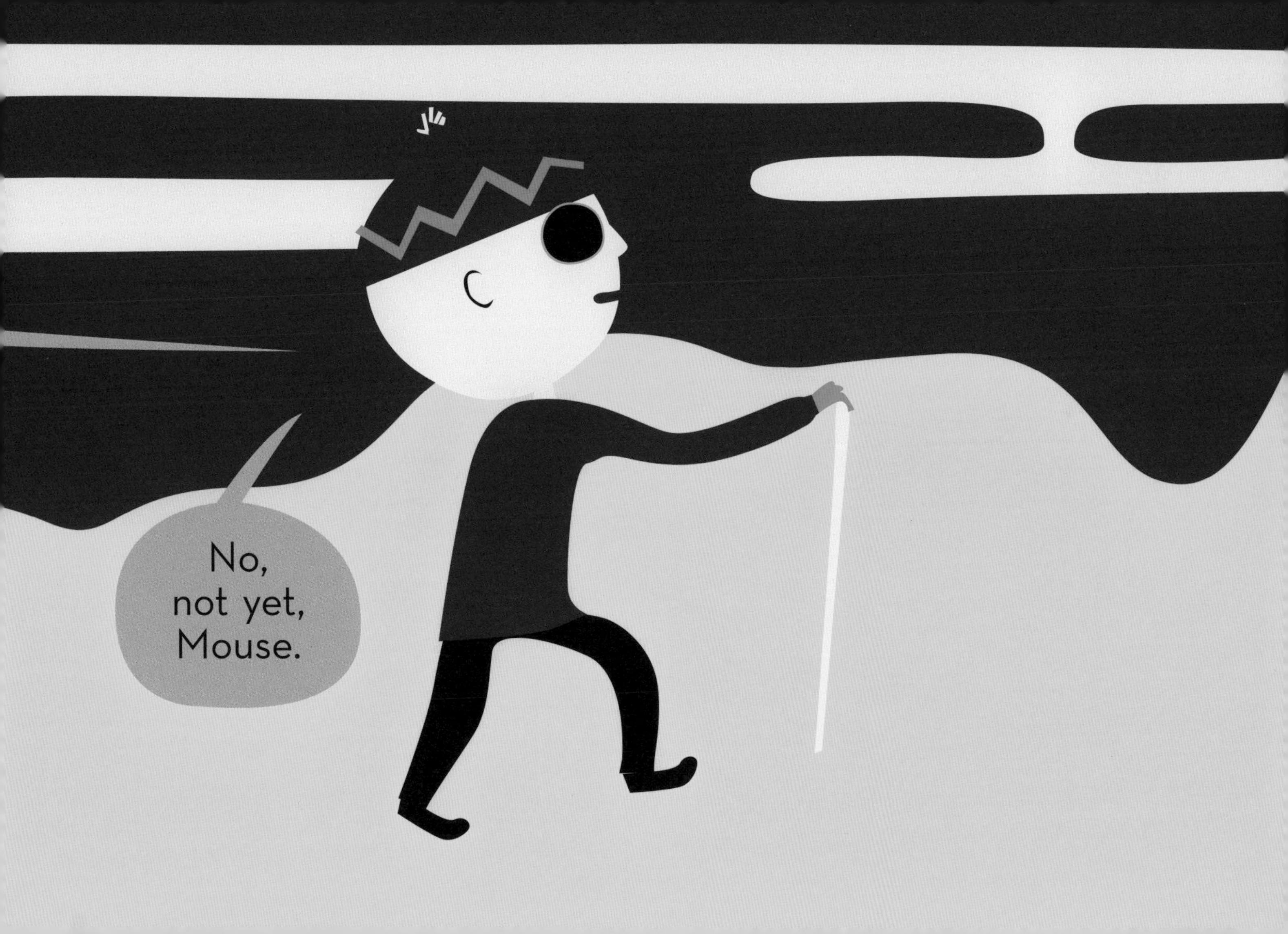
No, not yet, Mouse.

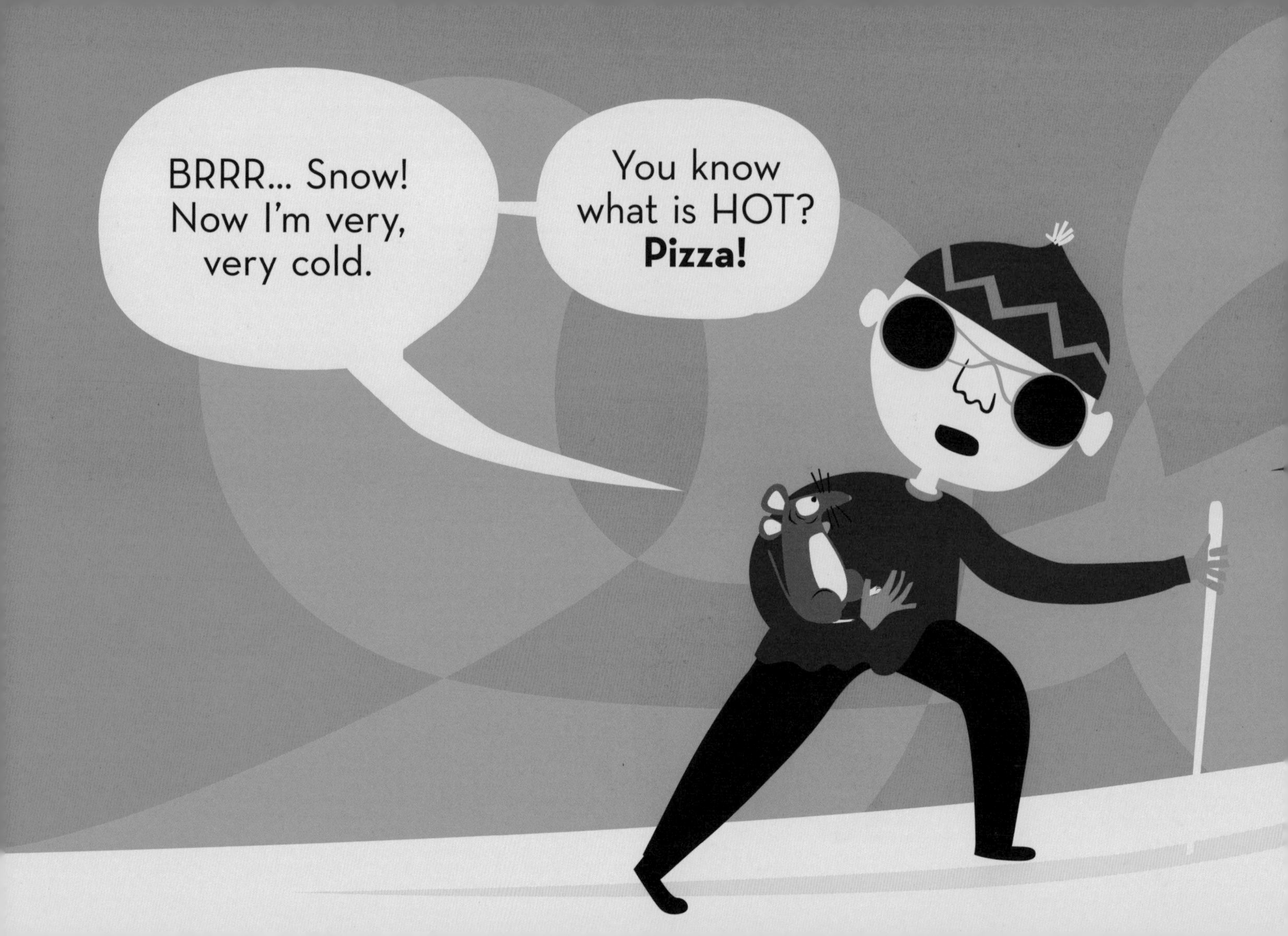
BRRR... Snow! Now I'm very, very cold.
You know what is HOT? **Pizza!**

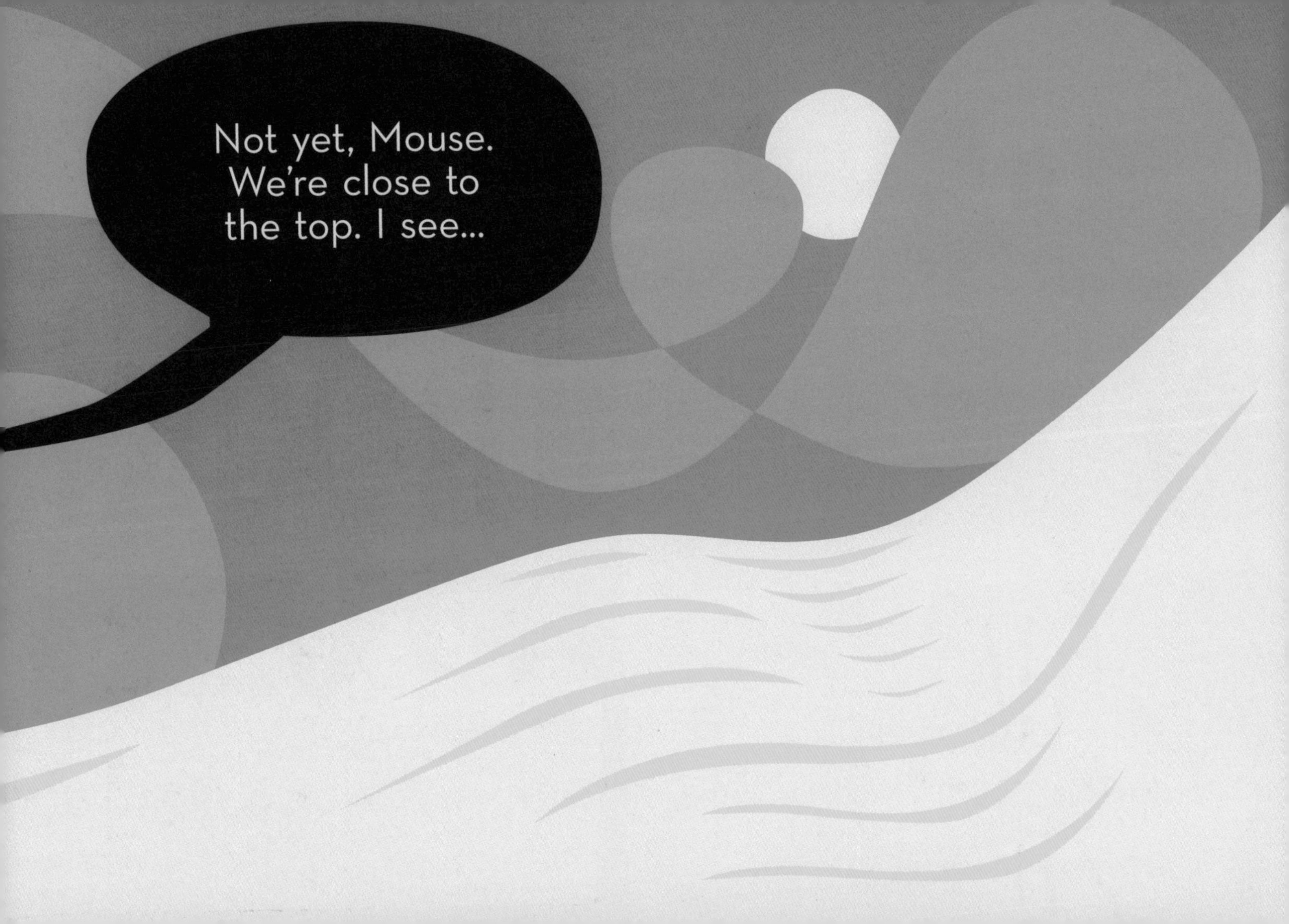
Not yet, Mouse. We're close to the top. I see...

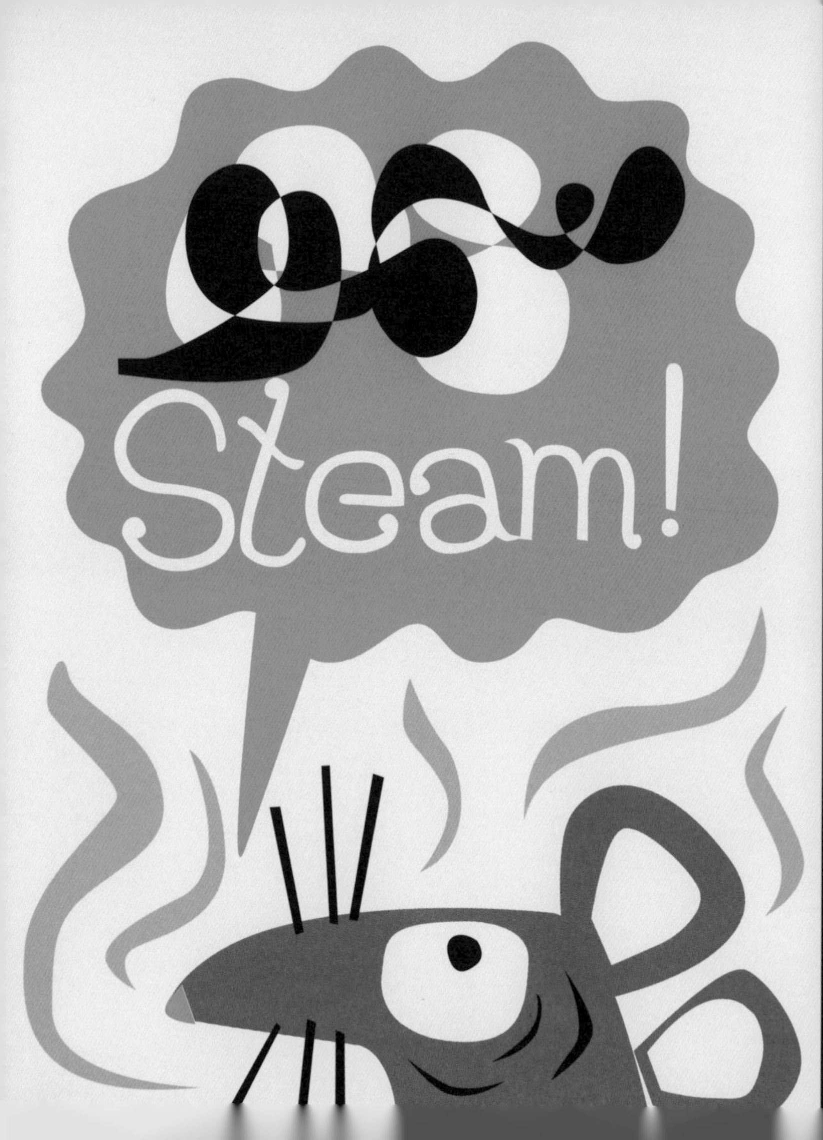
Steam!

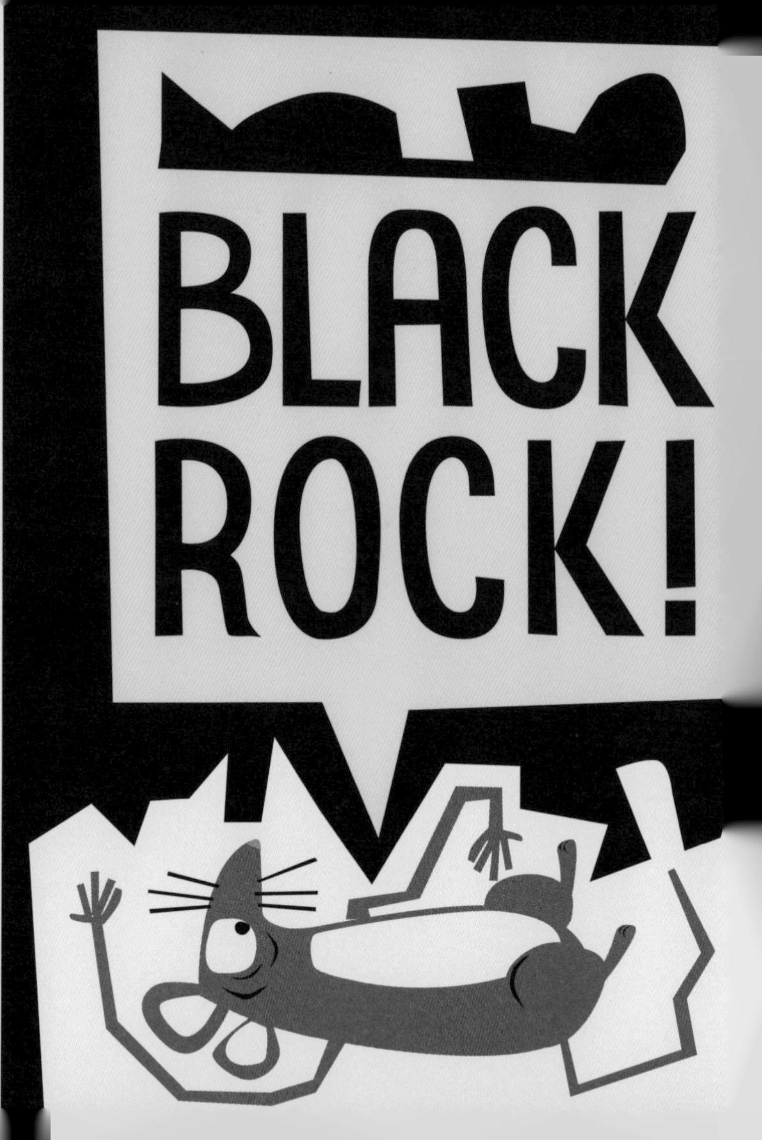
BLACK
ROCK!

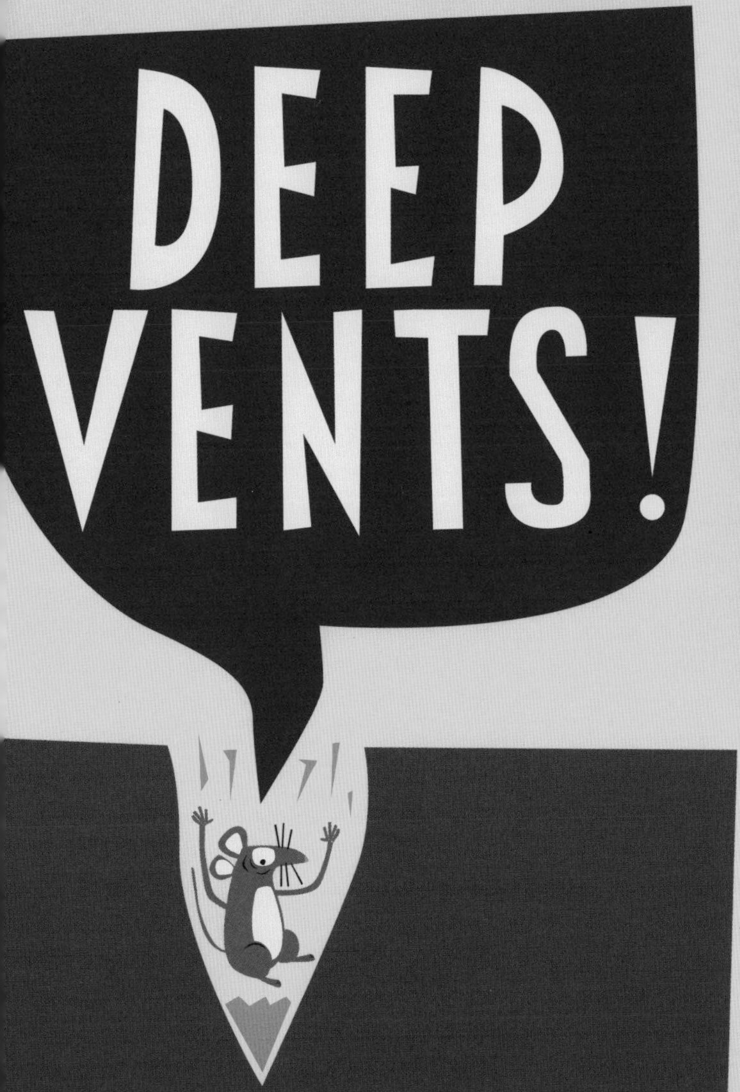
DEEP VENTS!

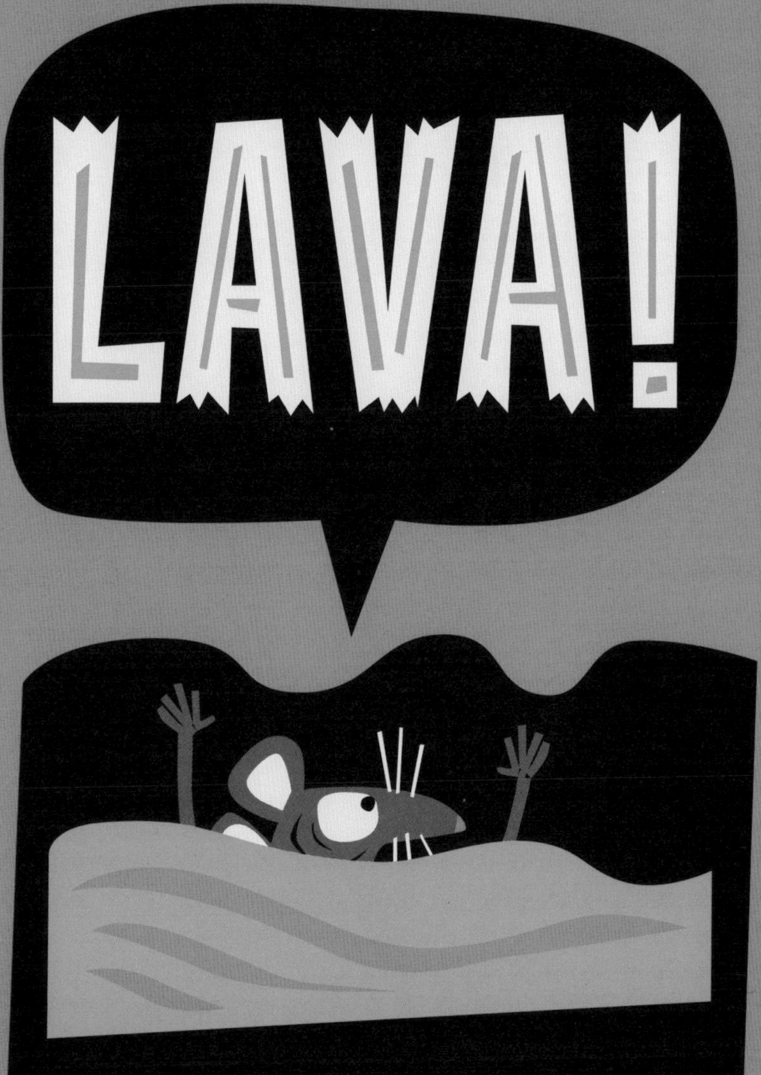
LAVA!

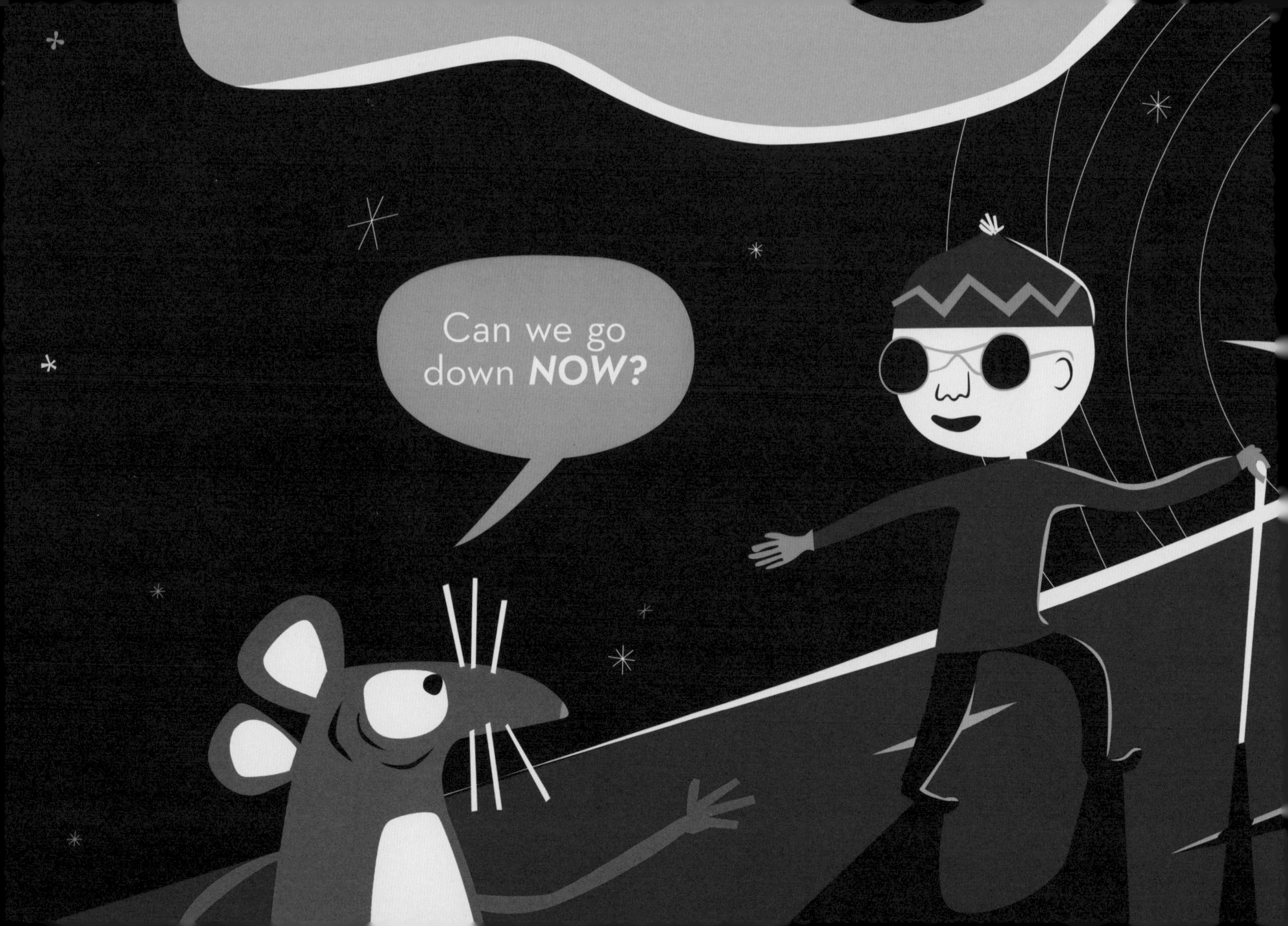
Can we go down **NOW?**

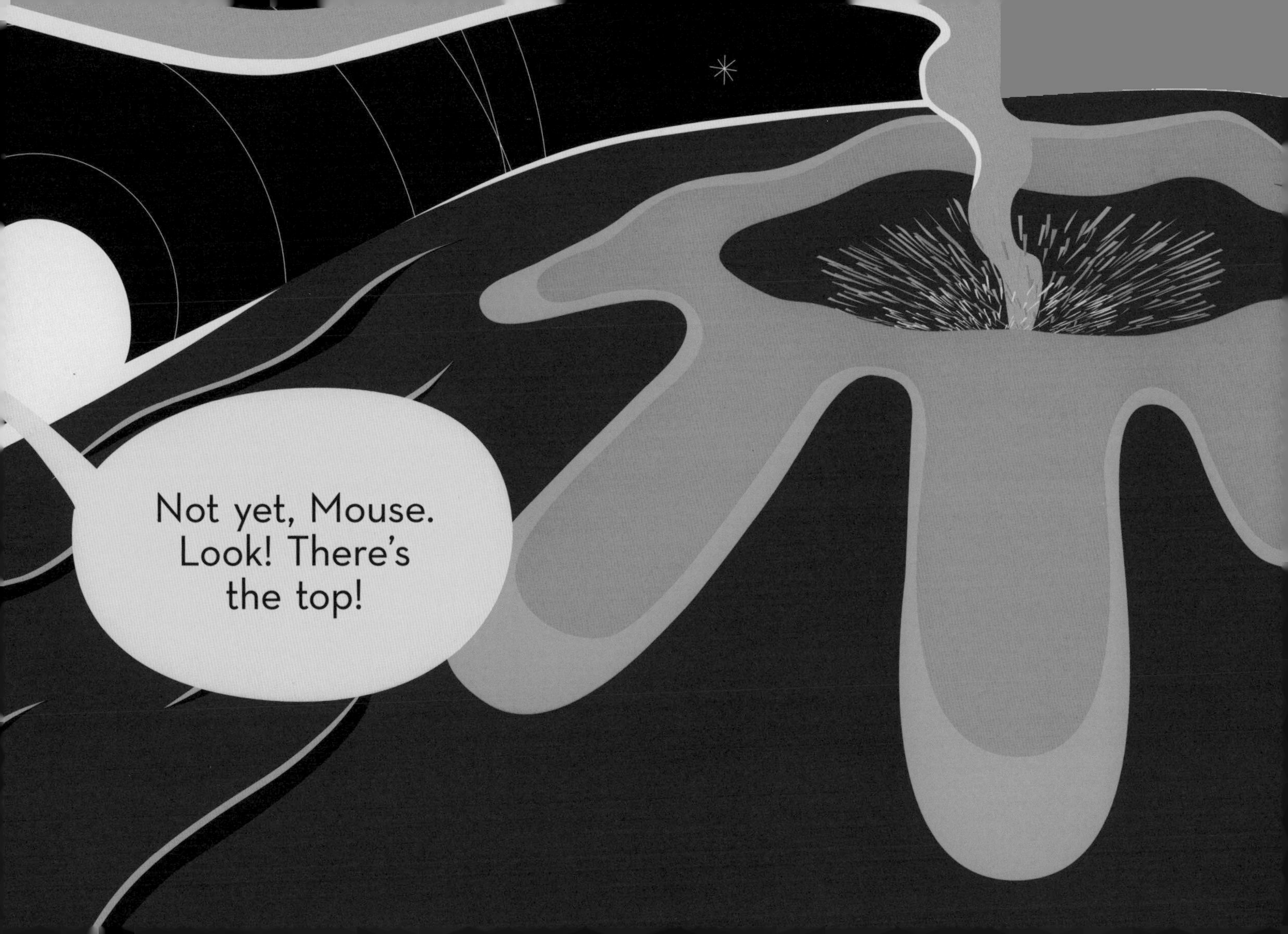
Not yet, Mouse. Look! There's the top!

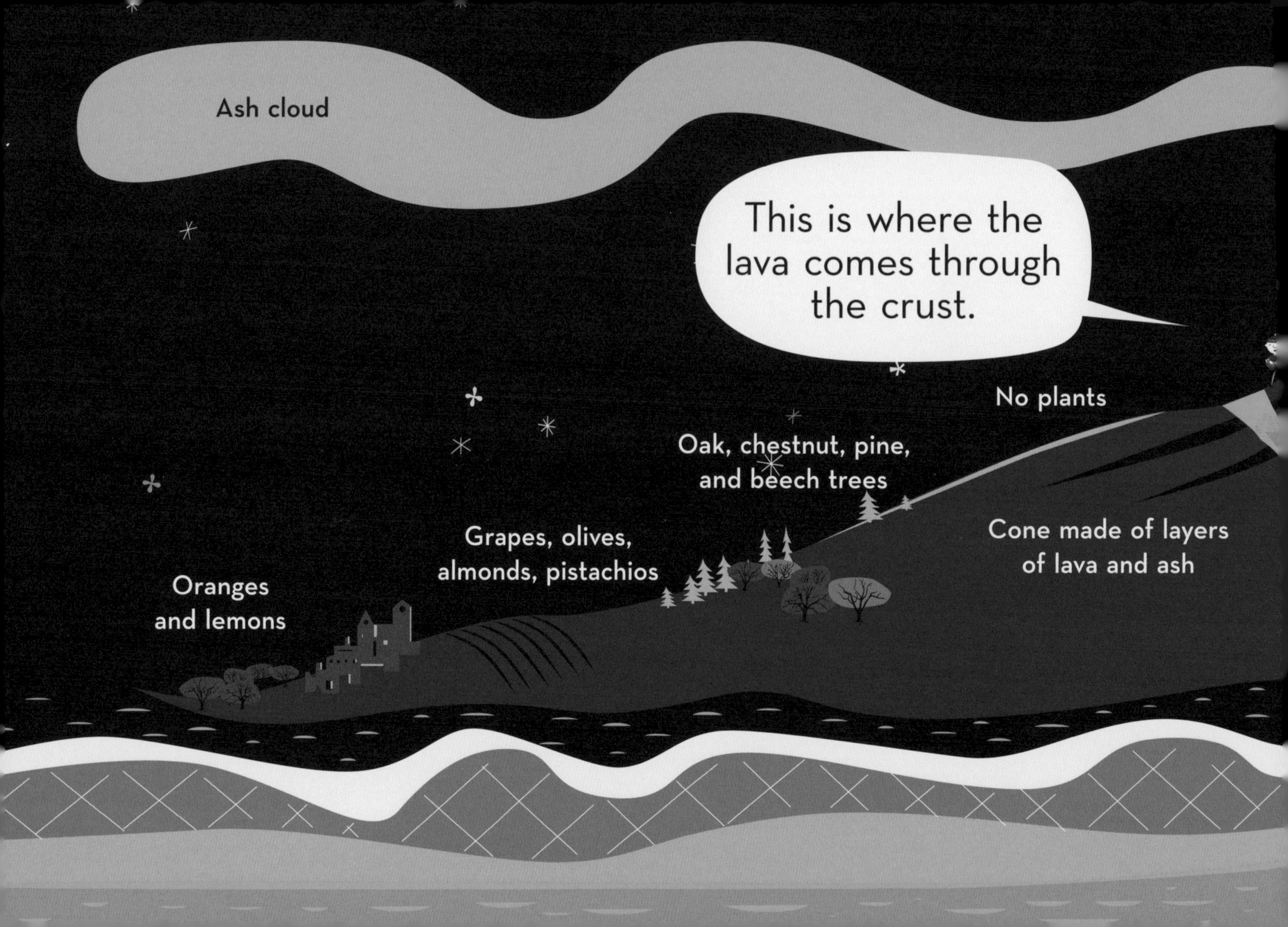
Ash cloud
This is where the lava comes through the crust.
No plants
Oak, chestnut, pine, and beech trees
Cone made of layers of lava and ash
Grapes, olives, almonds, pistachios
Oranges and lemons

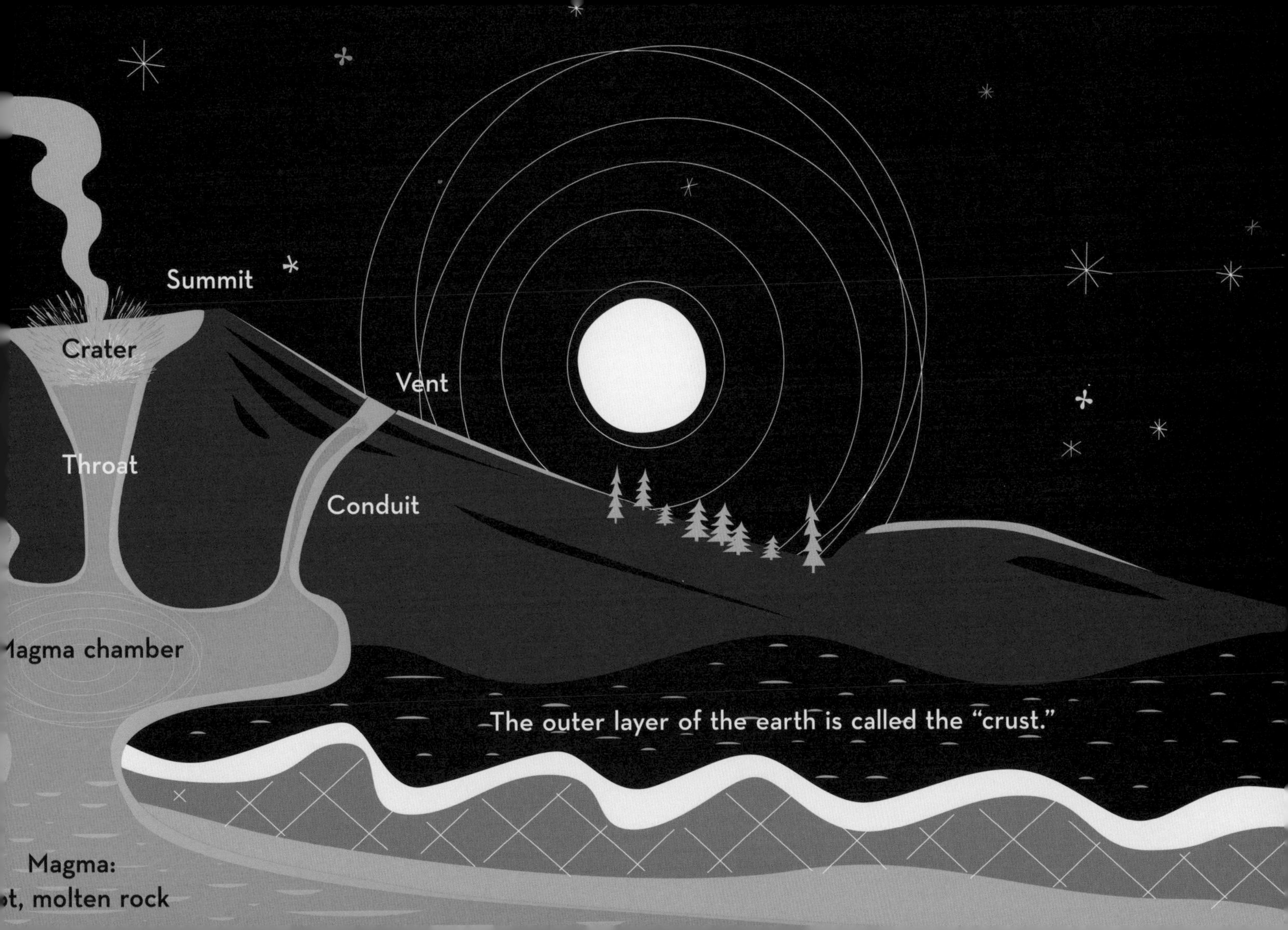
Summit
Crater
Vent
Throat
Conduit
agma chamber
Magma:
t, molten rock

The outer layer of the earth is called the "crust."

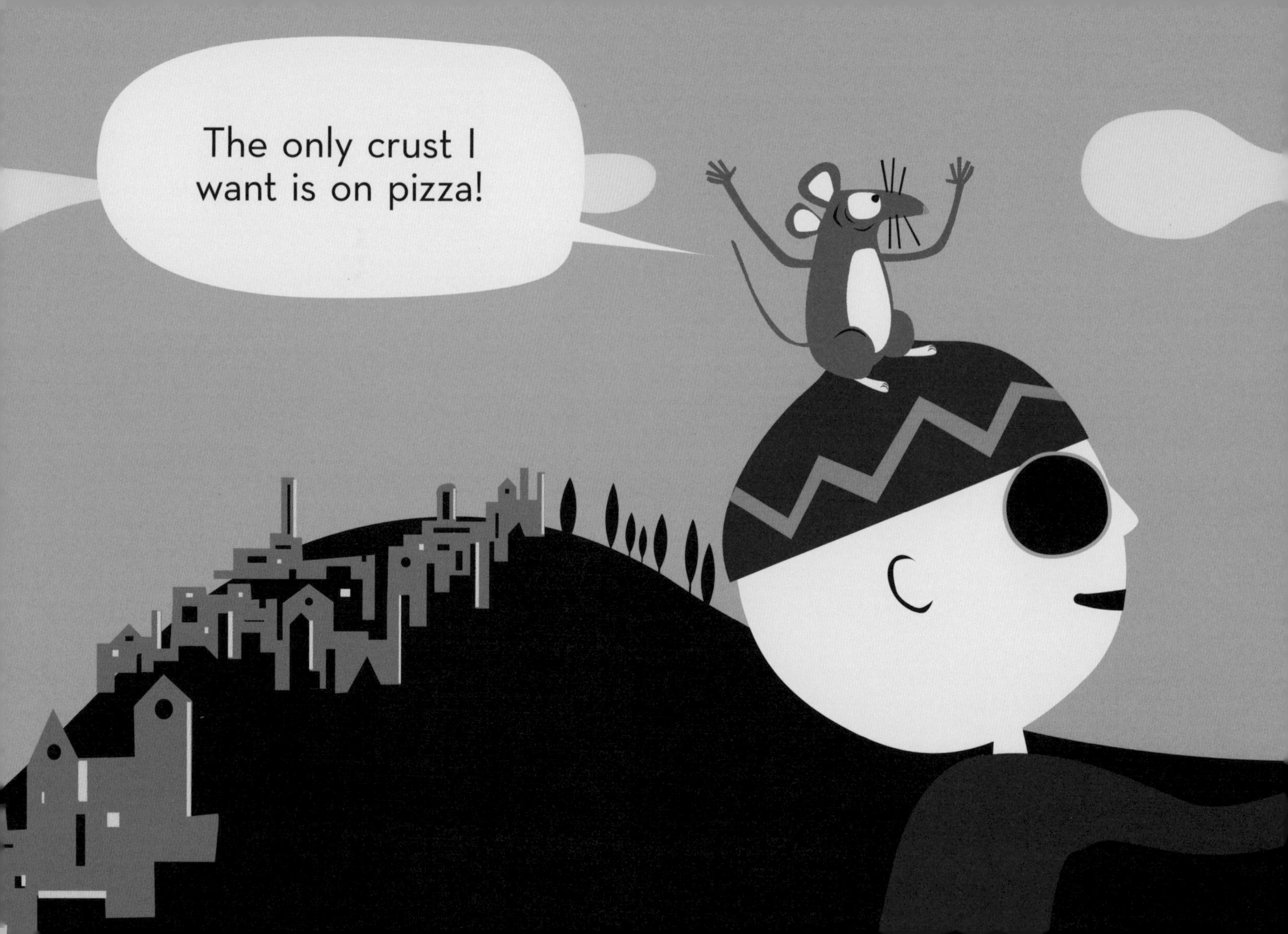
The only crust I want is on pizza!

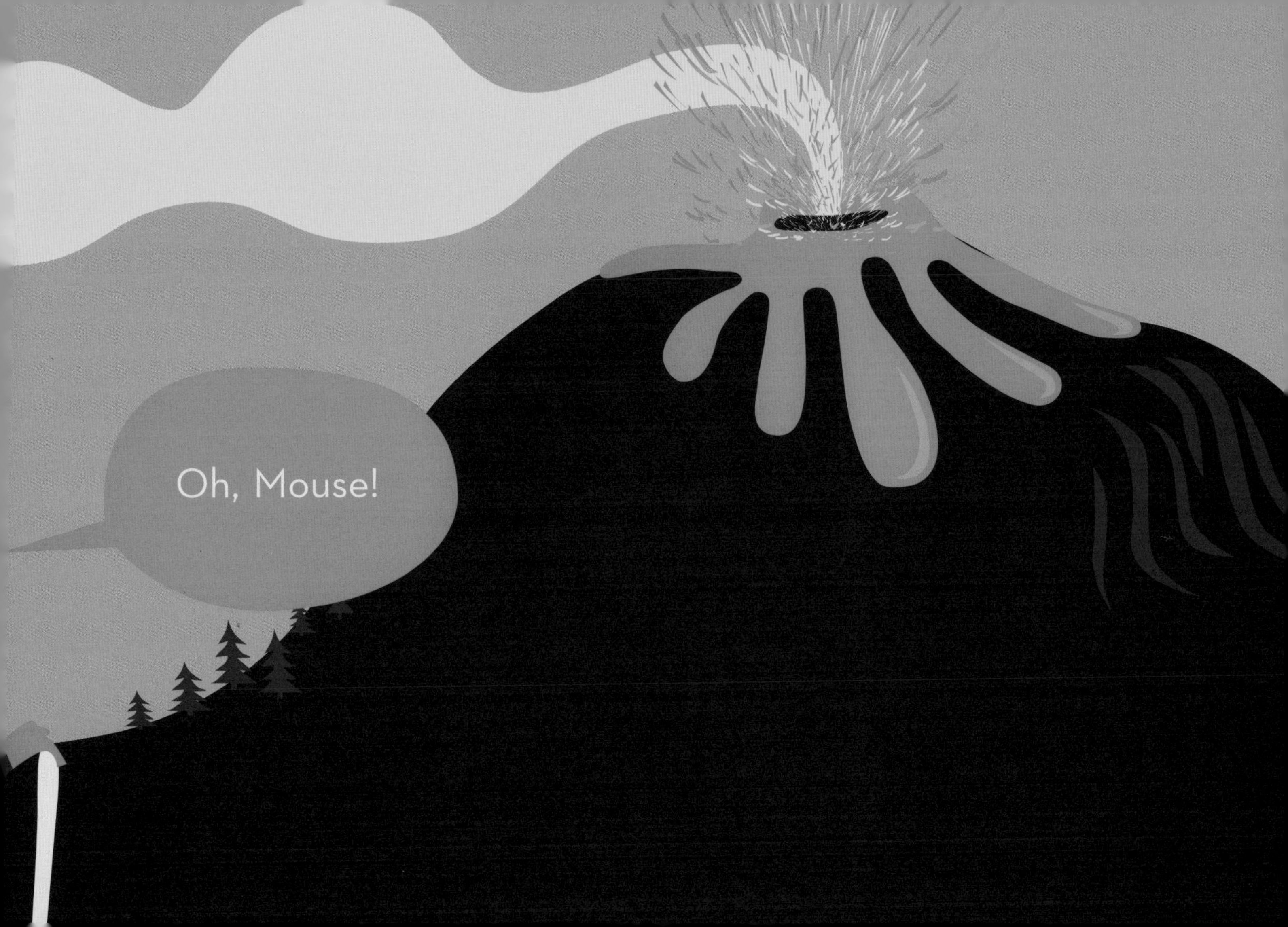
Oh, Mouse!

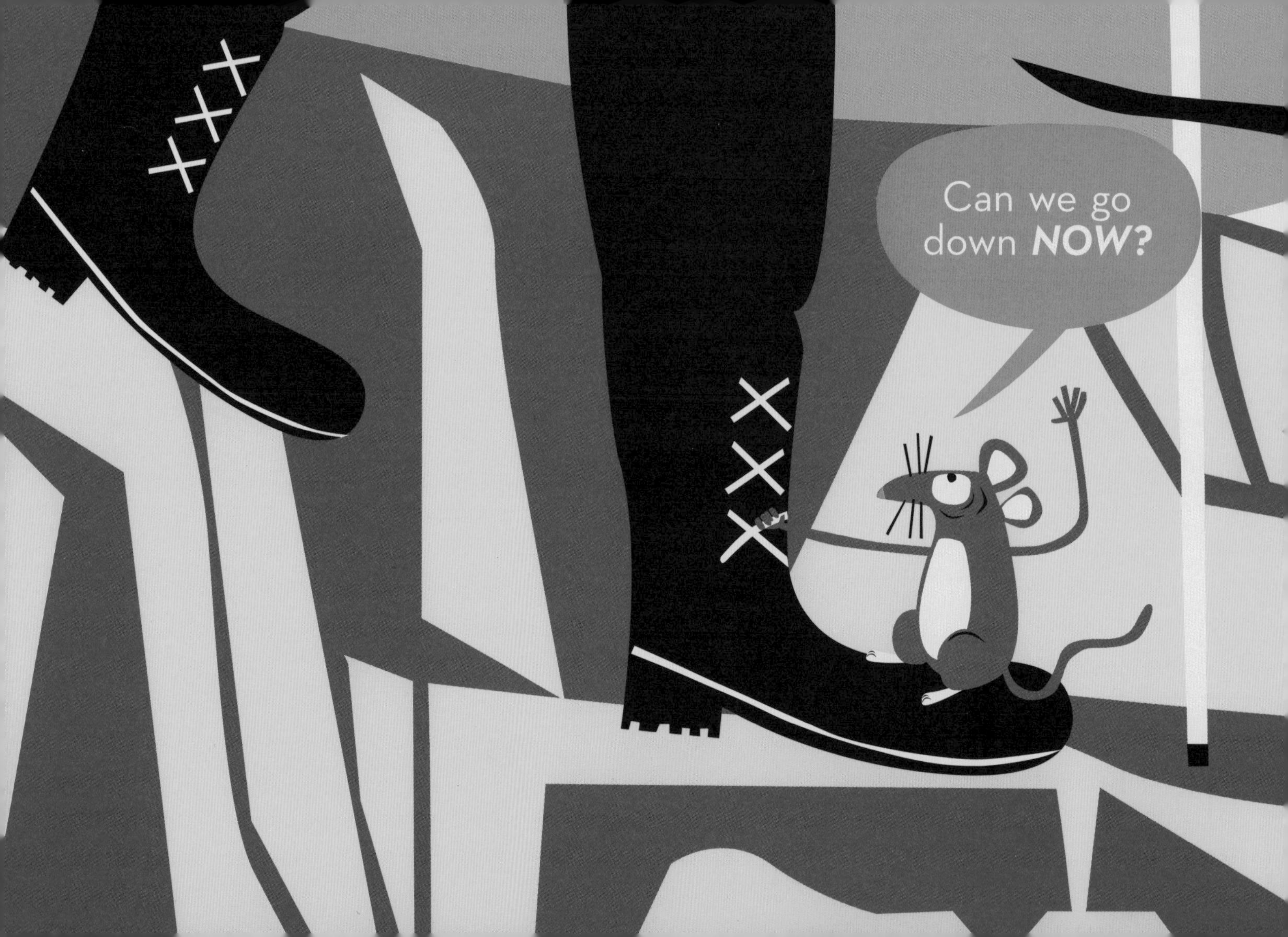
Can we go down **NOW**?

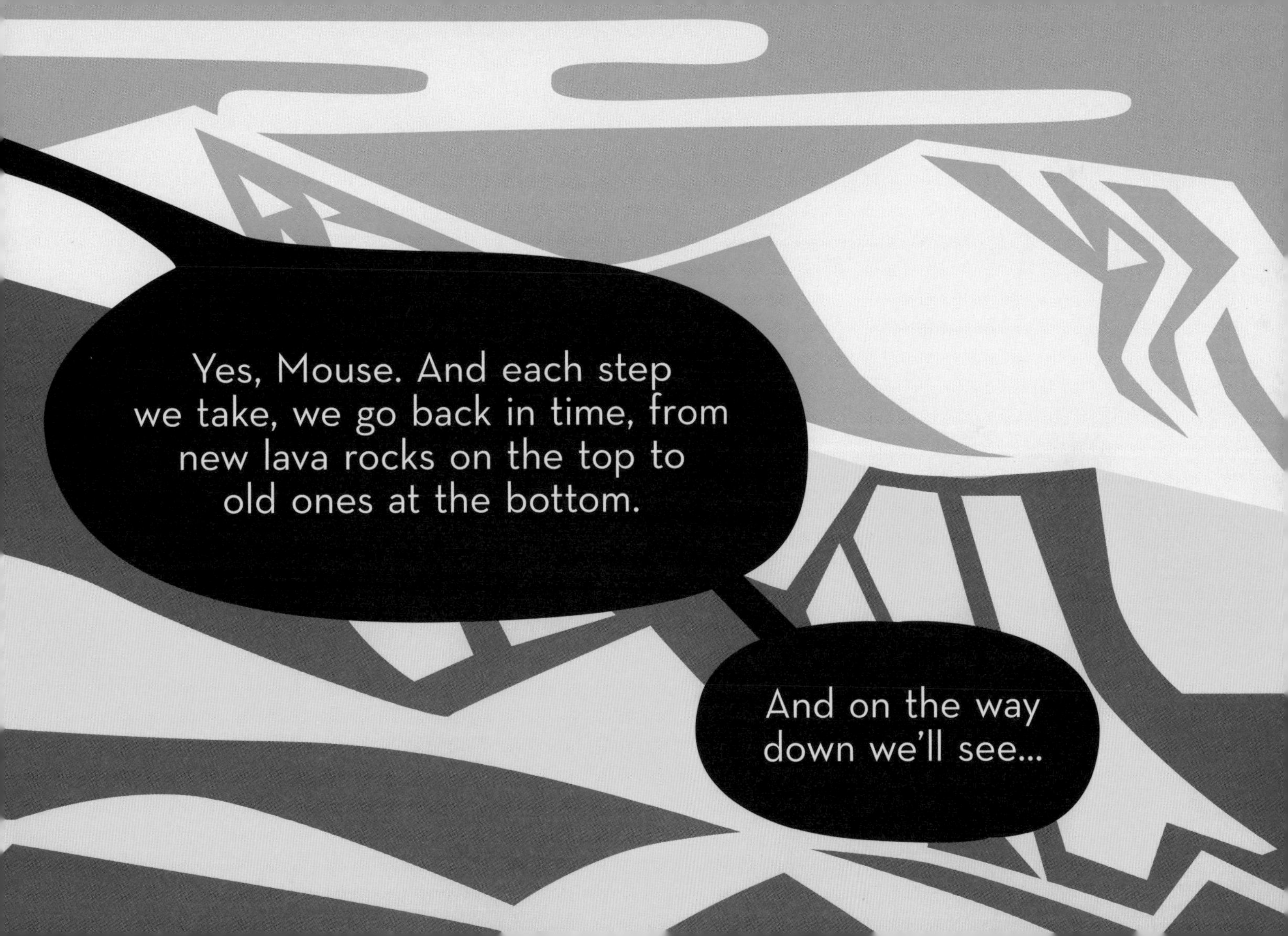
Yes, Mouse. And each step we take, we go back in time, from new lava rocks on the top to old ones at the bottom.
And on the way down we'll see...

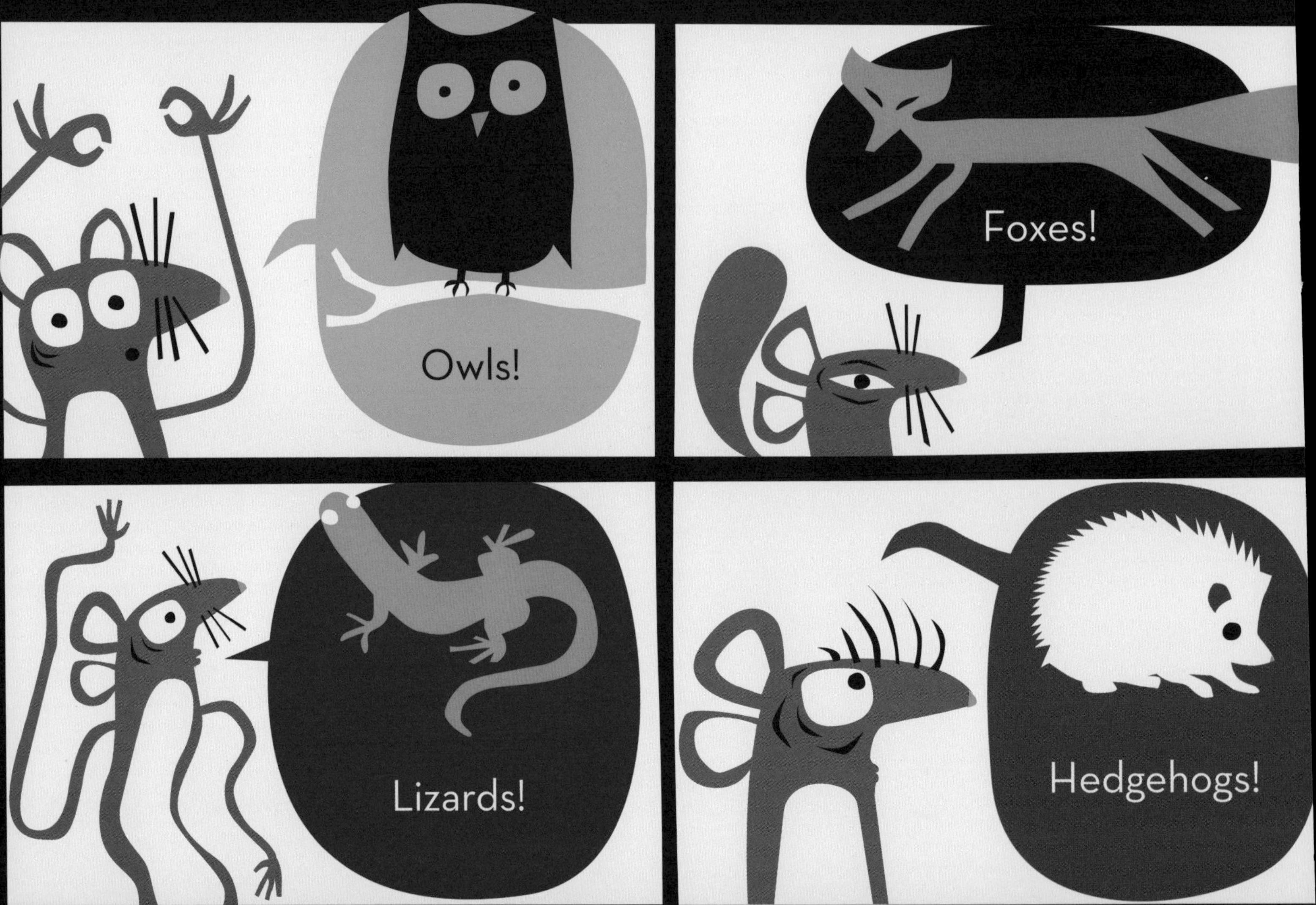
Owls!
Foxes!
Lizards!
Hedgehogs!

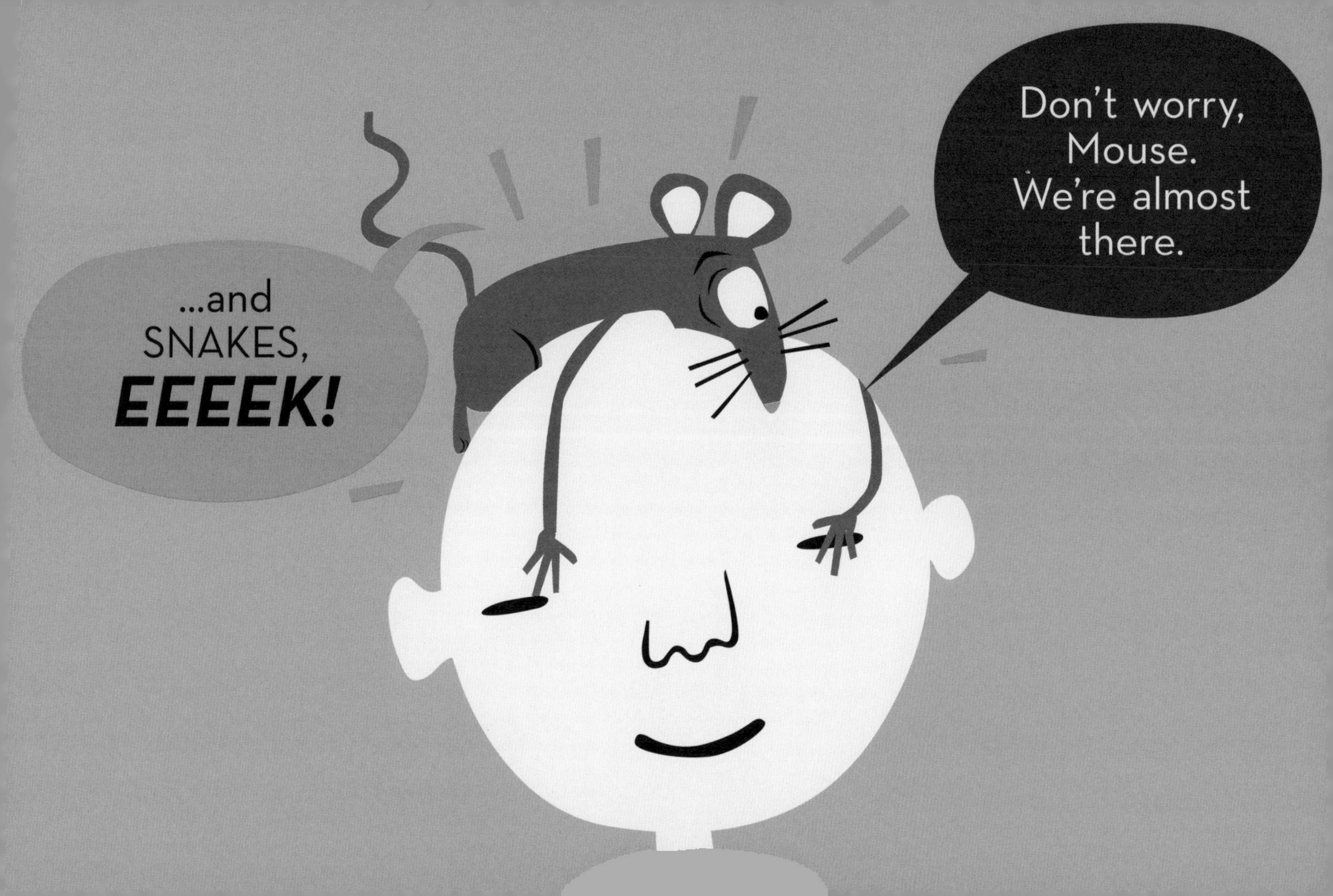
...and SNAKES, **EEEEK!**
Don't worry, Mouse. We're almost there.

# ABOUT THE AUTHOR

FRANK VIVA is an award-winning illustrator and designer who lives in Toronto, Canada. His art has appeared in prestigious places, such as *The New York Times* and the cover of *The New Yorker* – even in New York subway cars – but making children's books remains his favorite thing to do. He is known for the internationally acclaimed *Along a Long Road* (chosen by *The New York Times* as one of its Ten Best Illustrated Books), *A Long Way Away*, *Outstanding in the Rain*, *Sea Change*, and *Young Frank, Architect*. *A Trip to the Top of the Volcano* was born after Frank returned from a trip to Mount Etna in Italy: "Just back after two weeks in Sicily," he wrote us. "I climbed (over snow and lava) for hours partway up Mount Etna (and more hours back). We were with a vulcanologist and I learned a lot.  A Trip to the Top of the Volcano with Mouse? Just a thought." It's a companion book to *A Trip to the Bottom of the World with Mouse*, about Frank's experiences during a trip to the Antarctic Peninsula. Besides traveling, Frank is also passionate about cooking and eating. When his friends come over, he bakes them a delicious homemade pizza with a thin, crispy crust.

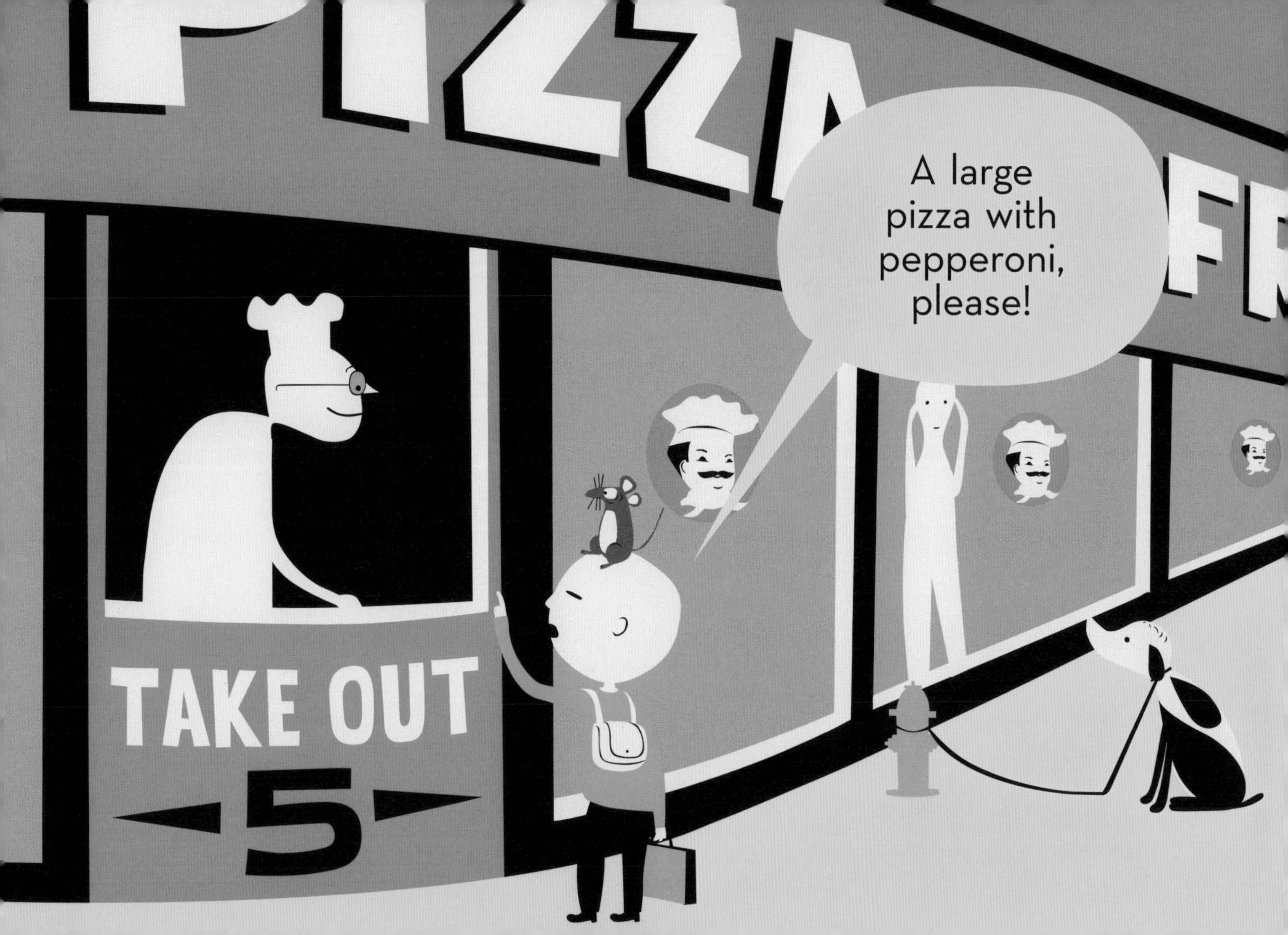
A large pizza with pepperoni, please!
TAKE OUT
5

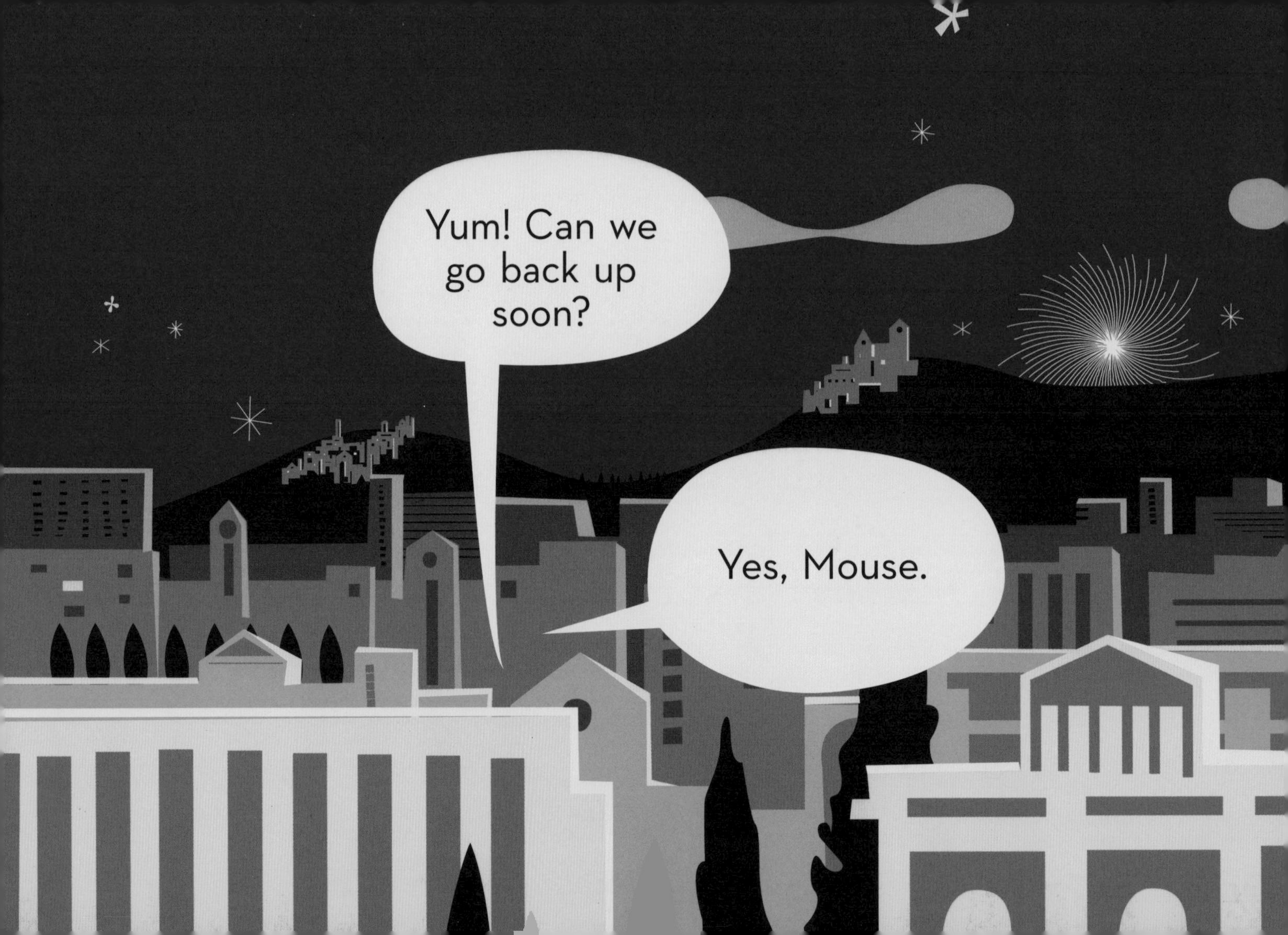
Yum! Can we go back up soon?
Yes, Mouse.